Bare

This is a work of fiction. Similarities to real people, places, or events are entirely coincidental.

BARE

First edition. June 10, 2024.

Copyright © 2024 Onyx Hart.

ISBN: 979-8224502691

Written by Onyx Hart.

To my sister, always being supportive and feeding my dirty little mind with ideas.

Love you, you kinky bitch.

Written by: Onyx Hart

Book 1

The Fatel Contractors Duet

This book has been entirely crafted by my imagination. None of the individuals are based on real-life people. It is important to know this book is a work of fiction, created solely for the enjoyment of reading.

I do NOT condone the actions of the characters in this book that are dealing with stalking, invasion of privacy, and shooting people.

It is a beautiful two-story house built in 1879 by one of the town's founders that is nearby. The house is about a mile from Kearney, Missouri, tucked in a small grove of white oak and silver maple trees, and sitting on 12 acres of land with a beautiful pond about 50 feet out the back door of the house. The drive from the road to the house is long and winding between the trees so it is not visible from the road but it's stunning to see in the fall as the leaves are turning. As you pull up to the house, it is white with red weathered shutters and has a beautiful wrap-around porch, with a second-story balcony off the master bedroom. The house is truly a sight to see at any given time of day or year.

The house is old enough I will have to gut it down completely to the bones and rebuild it to my liking yet still keeping era touches to not take from the integrity. I want to keep the house as close to the original beauty as possible but having it brought up to date is a must to make it livable.

I bought the house in disarray and found James Felden's company that same day to do all the work on the house. In the matter of 2 weeks, from the day I called to make the appointment with him, to the day I met him our fighting began and we seemed to have been butting heads.

But were we fighting over the house or something neither of us expected Things can turn around in the blink of an eye sometimes.

1

Molly

Today is the day I buy the house I have been waiting for, it's been for far too long and I am just hoping the house I want is for sale and in my price range. Waking up, I roll out of bed, taking a deep breath of the cool Missouri morning air and stretching. I'm a slender woman with the body of a runner, since I am one, with a light/fair complexion, and only five feet five inches tall. My brown wavy hair falls to the small of my back and gently over my shoulder. I only weigh 105 lbs, but I am stronger than I look. I run 15 miles a day for fun and I was in the military for six years.

I have always hated this area, growing up it was never enough for me so I left for the Navy as soon as I graduated. I couldn't leave fast enough, boot camp was a week after graduation. After six years I decided to get out of the military with an honorable discharge and come home to be with my family. We all have been through a lot and I felt like I needed my family. My mom had a heart attack a year ago and my dad could use the help around the house since she is still weak, though physical therapy has helped a lot. My dad can do it, but I would never forgive myself if I wasn't here for them. So, I came back home to help make it easier. My sister is also about three hours away, she comes as much as she can, but she has her own family to care for and I understand that. We have always been close, she is my best friend, but she is married with her own family, so I wanted to be here.

I didn't grow up poor, but we were not well off either. My parents were a typical blue-collar family, working hard for what we had but we never had it easy like other families may have. They worked for what we had and it got tight at times but mom and dad always made sure we had a good meal on the table, a roof over our heads, and clothes on our backs. As I grew up, I learned to invest and control my money. I wanted

4

to be able to have a little more freedom as I got older so now I spend my money wisely. I dress simply, nothing too expensive except a few outfits for the more formal dinners, parties, and major events that I may attend with my job, and I drive a 2009 Toyota Camry that I bought certified used in 2011 with one previous owner, it's in good shape, and well maintained wise low miles, I plan on keeping that until the wheels fall off which might take a while.

I have money though, my late fiancé, Kenneth, passed away from brain cancer in the middle of the night, only three months before we were due to be married. He knew he had it, but it spread too fast and there was nothing the doctors could do, and he never told me which broke my heart but I knew he wanted to spare me the worry. I met Kenneth through a friend when I was in the Navy, but when we were dating or even engaged, I didn't know he was a trust-fund baby. He had made me his sole beneficiary six months before the wedding date, leaving me 2.9 billion dollars. He was the last living member of his family, and I guess I was all he had.

I was beyond shocked and heartbroken when I received a letter saying that I needed to see his lawyer about his will, I had no idea what a lawyer would need to see me for, only two days after I buried him. I was only one of five people at his burial, the other four were friends of ours and it broke me more. He was an amazing man with a kind soul. He did so much to try and help everyone else, and not caring if the kindness ever came back to him, he was a pay-it-forward kind of man and I loved that about it, so selfless. I was more shocked and literally sick when I was given paperwork showing what he left me. Everything to his name, including a letter.

"Hello my love, I know I kept secrets from you and if you are reading this then I have passed before I was given a chance to tell you the truth. Honestly, I never wanted to tell you, I didn't want you to worry about me and stop living. You are so strong and amazing and I will always love you beyond words.. I want you to live, be happy, live for us both! I'm more

than sorry that I didn't tell you, and I wish I could change it, but my name was pulled and I was chosen to leave this earth. My family was the Mixton Family, they owned several businesses and holdings around the world, all of which I closed since I never wanted to be a part of the financial/political life. Corporate financial politics wasn't my thing, too corrupt. I know this money doesn't make you feel better, but I don't want you to want anything ever again! I want you to buy your house, the one you told me about in Missouri if you haven't already. Please know I am in a better place, and I will always be watching over you.

I Loved you with all my heart, always remember that
Till the day I died and beyond
Kenneth"

I cried so hard in the lawyer's office when I read the letter. The lawyer was so kind and patient, letting me sob like a madman for an hour before I could pull myself together. Kenneth was amazing and obviously had secrets.

Some of the secret experiences showed me that he wasn't the good boy everyone expected him to be, he had secrets that few knew about. He showed me that making love and fucking were very different, he was the only man I had ever been with. But he was good to me, no he was remarkably great, and I loved him more than words could explain. I decided I would follow his wishes even though it broke my heart.

I am going to buy my house using what money he left me. The family selling it was not expecting it to sell; they listed the house at $400,000 with the land which to me is a lot lower than it's worth for the land alone. Many people made offers above the asking price and the sellers kept turning them down from what my dad told me. I feel like they did it for a reason or maybe they weren't ready to part with the property yet. Something in me says that might change today though. It's an odd warm feeling but it's good, like luck is on my side for the first time in what seems like forever.

When I walked into the realtor's office and saw my dream house for sale I almost cried when I turned and asked for the realtor in charge of the Quartan House. The receptionist went and found a woman as I stood there and gathered my feelings. Now is not the time for me to cry. As the receptionist and another woman came around a corner from the back of the office and walked towards me I noticed not only her elegance but her natural beauty and I felt almost intimidated. God she is stunning. As she approached me, she extended her hand, and with a breathtaking smile that made me melt like never before, she said, "Hi, I'm Jazmine Kellen, you can call me Jaz. I hear you are inquiring about the Quartan House on Billings Lane?"

"Yes, I'm very interested in the house and have been for many years now. I am Molly Dowes." I said with a gracious smile trying to match her energy as I took her hand. She is like a stunning model and whereas I'm not ugly, she outshines me by far but her eyes draw me in. They are warm and welcoming even though they are almost ice blue.

Jaz is an amazingly beautiful woman. She is a stunning light-skinned black woman, with the brightest icey blue eyes and she styled her hair in simple tight curls that fall just past her shoulders. She is about five-eight and probably 130 lbs soaking wet but she is fit, with muscles in her legs like she runs. That makes me smile, maybe we could become friends and run together if she does.

We make small talk about the house and I tell her I am from the area as we turn to walk to her desk. As she walks slightly ahead of me, I notice the muscles in her legs with every step. I think my assumptions are right, those are runners' legs and I can't help but stare, I have never been attracted to women before but she is breathtaking.

She gestures to a simple desk with two pictures and two brown leather chairs in front of it. I follow her lead and take a seat in one of the leather chairs as she sits behind the desk and brings the property up on her computer. Turning the screen for me to look at, the pictures take my breath away.

The setting is unimaginably perfect, and the pictures of the pond with an enormous greenhouse behind the house were taken as the sunset light glistened off the water showing how well it has been taken care of and the small dock and patio closest to the house. The house and 12 acres are listed at $400,000, and the house needs so much work for sitting vacant for so long, it's a steal! At least if they will accept an offer.

"Now the house hasn't been lived in since around the 1940's, so it isn't in the best shape and needs a lot of work and updating. We have investigated the property history and there have never been any accidents involving a death on the property." Jaz explained as she scrolled through the pictures. "Would you like to set up a time to go see the house in person?" she asked with her warm smile, trying to hide the fact that she doesn't think the current owners will sell.

I smile back at her, almost laughing, "No, I have looked at that house since I was a teenager. I want it. I can make a cash offer immediately and can have the money in two hours if accepted."

Jaz looked almost puzzled by my response and looked me over wondering if I was going to be financing but then said, "Ok! That sounds great. How much would you like to offer? I will call the sellers now and pitch it to them to see what they think. I will say I can't tell you how much others have offered but the owners have denied everyone, I just want you to be aware of that beforehand so if they deny the offer you can already be prepared."

Without hesitation, "I would like to offer them $450,000 for the property." I see Jaz's smile falter just for a moment, I assume that's less than others have offered but we will see. The worst they can say is no and hopefully counter. My nerves are out of control making me jittery with anticipation, this has become the most real dream and I need to feel fulfilled.

I didn't tell her what I do yet, being the lead designer for an architect company, or that while I was in the Navy, I invested the majority of my money wisely and I only kept enough for food for two weeks and a few outings with friends twice a month. The rest of my money was kept in CDs, or other money-making ventures. I rarely lost anything I invested, so by the time I got out of the Navy, I had just under 1 million dollars, not to mention the $2.9 billion left to me by my late fiance in his will. Not all of that came from the military, they don't pay well enough for that kind of money, I had multiple jobs since I knew I wanted to buy THIS house one day and I always saved my money to do so.

After a few moments, I glance up from my phone as Jaz hangs up the office phone and begins to smile uncontrollably. I knew the words before they left her mouth. I began to vibrate with excitement feeling my palms get clammy, putting my cell on the desk, I started to rub them over my thighs.

"They accepted the offer, saying something about how they had been waiting for you since they knew you were coming home, something about your dad telling them you were coming home." she exclaimed with the brightest smile and a slight questioning look lighting up her eyes.

"I should have known he would have casually mentioned it to them." I laugh as I tell her "I knew today was going to be a good day. I'll head over to the bank and get the money. Will the paperwork be ready today or do you need more time?" I ask knowing all too well that it will be ready in a couple of hours.

"Yes, everything will be in order for you in about 2 hours." She smiled, you could see the excitement in her eyes as she was trying not to jump for joy. This must be a big achievement for her too and that makes me happy to be a part of.

"Well, I will see you in two hours then.." I say as I stand from my seat, shaking her hand, and all but run out the door of the office. My hands are still clammy and I feel like I am about to hyperventilate with the excitement thrumming through me.

Looking to the sky, I feel a single tear slide down my cheek, "We did it, babe, I wish you were here to grow in this house with me." I whisper, barely loud enough to hear. Looking back down at the town in front of me, I whip the tears from my eyes, taking a deep breath to calm myself, and let the biggest smile spread across my face as I call the bank.

I informed the bank manager that I was coming and told them what I needed so when I got there, I just had to sign some paperwork and the money was ready in about 15 minutes. I took the extra hour and a half to investigate contractors since I knew I would need a professional for this house. Yes, my dad and I could do some of the work, but I don't feel like fighting with him over every decision I want to make, and we can't do a lot of the work without a crew.

I head to a local coffee shop, pull my tablet out of my purse, and open Google to start searching for contractors. I looked up highly rated contractors within a 50-mile radius and was surprised at how many popped up. The fourth one on the list caught my attention for some reason though, R2R Construction has over 1500 five-star reviews and only two reviews were four stars for the lead contractor having an attitude. That makes me laugh, a challenge sounds fun right about now.

I decided to call the number, and immediately my call was answered by a woman who sounded to be in her 40s or 50s, she had a pleasant voice and you could hear the smile in her tone through the phone, "Rags2Riches Construction, this is Alice, how may I help you today?"

"Hello Alice, my name is Molly Dowes. I am about to sign the papers on the Quartan House over on Billings Lane. I would like to make an appointment with the head contractor to meet at the house and get a rough appraisal on renovation cost." I know the more firm I sound, the more serious they will take me since I am a woman and women tend to be walked all over on construction sites. I see it happen at work all the time, so I make sure I am clear but not rude.

Alice takes a moment before answering, assuming she is looking at the schedule, "Sounds like you have made a wonderful investment, congratulations. James Felden is the Owner of the company, he will want to go through this process with you, renovating old homes is a secret passion of his and he has been eyeing that house for about two years now." I can hear her joy as she shares a little information about him like a secret. "It looks like he has an opening next week on Thursday at 2 pm, does that work for you?" The offered appointment time came off as scripted or robotic.

"That would work perfectly, I plan on being there most of the week anyway." I exclaim as I write the date, time, and with whom I will be meeting on a piece of paper to add to my calendar.

Alice went on to explain that the appointment would take about three hours since the property is so large, which I expected, and she informed me that if I canceled without a minimum of a three-day notice, my name would be blacklisted from the company ever working with me again. Seems a bit extreme but ok, I roll my eyes at her comment but I don't let it bother me too much, I know she is just the messenger.

I know this information was meant to warn me against canceling except for emergencies, but it didn't, more so annoyed me. I was free all week, and I planned on being at the house most of the time with samples of different items to try and make this process easier in the long run.

I agree to the conditions and confirm the appointment time before ending the call.

As I stroll into the office, Alice greets me with a warm smile as she always does. She always has this motherly smile and inviting nature to her, that's why I hired her when I started R2R five years ago. She makes people feel welcome, whereas I seem to make people feel uncomfortable. I wasn't raised to be a soft man so it doesn't bother me, I tend to not like people much and I only tolerate the people I have to work with because they pay me or I pay them.

Alice is an amazing woman in her mid-sixties, she has a head of completely gray hair but her figure is more of a woman in her late 30's. She is petite, especially for having 5 children and 11 grandchildren. All her kids joined the service out of high school, including her only daughter whom she still worries about but she is proud of them all. I always make it a point to ask how they are all doing, although I have never met any of them. I know it makes her happy to talk about them, and the more she talks about them, the less she asks about me or my past which I hide from everyone. Alice has figured that out over the years and she doesn't ask as much but now and then she will.

"Good morning Alice, how are you today? Oh and did Kade receive the promotion?" I ask as I close the door to the office behind me and begin to take off my jacket. Kade is her oldest son in the Marine Corps, I think.

"Morning James, I'm well today thank you for asking. And yes Kade did receive his promotion, he is officially a Gunnery Sergeant." She proclaims with a huge smile as she hands me a cup of black coffee in one hand and a stack of notes and messages in the other.

I took the morning off, so it is already 11 am by the time I get in when I usually get here at 5 am, but she knows how I am about my coffee and always has a fresh pot for me when she knows I will be in the office. I knew I would have a list a mile long of potential clients to call back since it's a buying market right now.

Not knowing I was up all night railing into my neighbor's sister, I needed the caffeine to pick me up since I had to get Janey out of my house. She is cute but clingy and I needed to clean up before I came in so I didn't stop for coffee. I think that was her name at least, I smiled to myself. I don't do relationships, they complicate things so I just fuck whoever I want and send them on their way the next morning.

The first note in the stack gets my attention quickly, 'Molly Dowes bought the old Quartan house. Scheduled meeting for complete reno Thursday, the 10th at 2 pm' I read aloud as I turned back around and I can feel my eyes almost pop out of my head as I look back at Alice. She doesn't usually make appointments without talking to me first, but she knew I wanted to remodel this house so she must have made it knowing I would be upset to lose this opportunity..

"The Quartan house sold to a woman?" I almost yell before I have fully turned around.

But as I turn to fully face her, I notice Alice smiling from ear to ear, "Yes sir, the woman seems like a lovely girl over the phone and since I know you have wanted to renovate that house since you found the place a couple years ago, I made time in your schedule. You be nice to her, I know you usually like dealing with men on the jobsite but she seemed sure of herself and I think you want this job more than you want to be a jerk." She always scolds me before I speak with women. In construction, they don't usually know enough to be more than a nuisance and I enjoy making them feel belittled. I know it is wrong but it always makes me smile like the devil I am.

I swear Alice is the only woman that can be frank with me like that and I won't get mad at her. She reminds me of my Aunt Penny back in Boston, before she had a massive stroke and passed away.

If Alice knew who I was and what I'm capable of, she would run straight to the police or her sons and I wouldn't blame her. That's one reason I never told her, the other reason is more complicated and dangerous. She brings peace into my life though. Even as she infuriates me, she is warm and caring in a way I never knew possible till I met her.

I roll my eyes because I do hate working with women. They never really know anything about construction. The rich ones flirt, and sometimes I may sleep with them, but overall I prefer to work with men, they are easy to intimidate, but most of the men don't know how to thread a pipe properly so I guess there isn't much to say there either. Thinking, I roll my eyes to myself again.

The people that hire me are rich like they have too much money and they don't know what to do with it all. I've been there so I get it but it still annoys me. So this "girl" is a surprise. She must be a trust-fund baby, though I have no room to talk, I had a $15 billion inheritance that I cleared out to start over with.

She won't know her ass from her elbow and I'm already rolling my eyes at the idea of having to speak with her let alone do a full walk-through of that entire house with her. Watch she will show up afraid to get her shoes dirty and will whine like a little bitch the entire time. I can feel it in my bones and that is why I hate working with women on the jobs, I don't have time to deal with their shit.

I will just reject the appointment, maybe say I don't have time. Although I really wanted to remodel that house, I guess I will have to pass and take the internal battle I will have, or I could just steamroll her like I would any other woman and get my way. Both are good ideas. I will just have to see how she acts when I call.

I look up to notice I'm still standing in the front of the office and Alice is giving me her "you're not canceling this appointment," look and I roll my eyes letting out a sigh. Realizing I have been standing here thinking about this dilemma. She knows me too well sometimes and as much as it makes me mad, I know she means well and her connections around the area have helped groom this business to what it is in just the five years I have been here.

I turn to walk into my office to get started on calls and research for appointments I intend to keep.

"James, I swear to the good lord above and the demons below, if you think you are canceling that appointment because it is with a woman, I will help you meet your maker faster than you expected." I hear Alice exclaim as I am already shutting the door and shaking my head. I can't help but smile once my door is shut. As much as I know she is joking, she also makes me think about her words. She can be a mean old bat when someone has pissed her off.

I designed my office very simple since I am on the job sites more than I am here. I have an old antique desk that Alice's great grandfather made back in 1845. She gave it to me as a grand opening gift when I started this business and I never thought I would love and appreciate a piece of furniture like I do this. She said she was going to sell it anyway since her kids didn't want it, so I was honored to have a piece of her family since she has become a part of mine. In front of the desk is 2 leather chairs, much like you find at an old doctors office, they aren't comfortable or welcoming since I don't like people to linger, and on the other side of the room, the wall is nothing but a huge quirk board pinned with notes, ideas, and samples for ongoing sites my crews are working at, the quirk board is above a massive drafting table that I had built for the office, it extends from wall to wall so I have plenty of space to work on multiple projects at once.

I sit behind my desk, looking through the notes and messages from people who work for me but I keep coming back to the first one. "Molly Dowes" I mutter to myself, "who are you?"

Looking at my computer, my hands start typing before I can think, and I am searching her name for any information I can find. She has social media, but nothing about her screams 'I have money'. She is an ordinary girl. From the area, social media tells me that her fiancé died from cancer, she is 28 and doesn't have any kids. But fuck me she is stunning. She isn't tall, but she is fit, and her hair, and I can easily imagine twisting it into my fist as I bend her over my desk. I bet she is tight and needy, I think to myself and I can feel my cock start to wake up. I palm the bulge, urging it to go down. Focusing on work instead of her beautiful bright eyes.

Why would she want a house this big? I can't help but wonder about her. She is actually beautiful, in an ordinary kind of way. There is nothing overly remarkable about her in her pictures, but she has those eyes that light up the darkest parts of me, like they could mend my black soul. She is not someone I need to get comfortable with. She could ruin everything I am avoiding, but I can't help but want her. Something calls me to her.

I have made up my mind as I pick up the phone and dial the number she left with Alice.

She answers on the second ring, "Hello" and fuck me she has a voice that can melt ice and smooth over any rough edge.I cleared my throat, ignoring the bulge in my pants again that decided it liked her voice much more than I expected.

"Hello, is this Molly Dowes?" I ask with as much of a brute tone as I can muster but I also work to keep my voice board.

"Yes, and this is?" She says it with such sass, I can feel more blood rush to my cock as I bounce my leg, god I want to spank that tone out of her and I don't even know her but I can feel my blood boiling.

"This is James Feldon from Rags 2 Riches Construction. I was just calling to let you know unfortunately, Alice didn't know I wouldn't be able to do a walk-through next week. I am completely booked for the next 12 months so I won't be able to help with your renovation of the Quartan house." Drumming my fingers on my desk with a cocky smirk, knowing I won.

She laughs, and not a funny laugh, it's almost a backhand across my face as I feel my expression shit from a smirk to shock. "I have heard that you tend to cancel appointments with women," she starts but I cut in.

"That's not…" is all I get out before she gets snappy with me and I am shocked at how she commands attention and respect.

"I'm sorry I wasn't done speaking and I let you speak so you WILL give me the same respect. Now, as I was saying I heard you tend to do this with women, and since you are supposed to be the best in the area anymore, I want your company to do my house and I promise I'm not an easy woman to say no to. You aren't going to intimidate me into doing anything I don't want including canceling this meeting, and I already have what I need in my head. If you think money is an issue, I assure you it isn't. With that being said, I will see you next Thursday at 2 pm." There is a long pause, "Now you may speak."

I can feel the shock deep in me as I stare at the phone like it might be a ghost. Holy fucking hell, I've never been spoken to like that by anyone let alone a woman and I am completely thrown off and hard as I notice my cock in my pants trying to bust threw the zipper. I take a deep breath, clearing my head of wanting to fuck that smart mouth out of her. How does she do this to me before I have even met her?

"Don't be late or I will turn around and never come back." I growl as I hang up the phone with a slam much harder than necessary. Frustrated and horny now, from only her fucking voice, what the fuck! I haven't had this happen since I was a teen and hit puberty.

What the fuck just happened? How the fuck did her smart mouth and the silky heat of a voice get under my skin? She is making me do what she wants, no one has ever gotten me to do what they want, they do what I want, ALWAYS.

Sitting back against my chair, I palm my throbbing cock through my pants a few times before I decide I need to pull out the research, plus Alice doesn't need to walk in on me stroking my cock. That would not only be unprofessional but mortifying since she is like a mother. Turning back to my file cabinet, I pull the file with the research I have done on the Quartan House, making a new label for it 'Molly Dowes-Quartan House'.

Rolling my neck, I have to get Molly Dowes as far out of my head as I can before finishing my other work. Taking a deep breath I work on thinking of things that calm me so I can focus on work.

3

Molly

Today is the day I officially meet James Felden, although he TRIED to cancel on me, arrogant asshole. I have been at the house since 7 am, walking the property, seeing what trees are dead and need to be removed, inspecting the greenhouse, and just taking in my new home. The house originally has five bedrooms and three and a half bathrooms with a great room, parlor, formal dining room, and a massive kitchen.

Kenneth would be so proud of me and that makes my heart almost hurt but I smile because I know I am doing the right thing. I walk to the back of the house to sit on the pier, overlooking the large pond, and just breathe in the beauty and forget the world around me while I soak up the sun.

At 2 pm on the dot, my phone reminds me to drink some water. I hear a vehicle at the front of the house and I roll my eyes at the thought of his attitude on the phone.. I get up and walk around the front of the house to see a brand new Dodge pickup coming up my driveway.

This must be James, play nice. We need him to help us, so don't be a bitch. I tell myself.

Before I can let the inner monologue process, James is stepping out of his truck. I look at my watch, "Hmm, 2 minutes late." I snarked at him with a coy smile, he already rubbed me the wrong way and I felt the need to get the first word in, but as he raised one eyebrow not seeming amused, I felt like a bug that just ran in his way with the cold dismissive look on his phone.

James is a large man that stands around six-six and he is pure muscle if the tightness of his clothes tells me anything. He must be a solid 280lbs of stacked, defined muscle, and you can tell he works out a lot, even while running a successful construction business that he not only owns but he has no problem being out on the job every day working with his employees, as my research told me. He has the most mesmerizing green eyes and jet-black curly hair, though you would never know unless he let it grow but I can see the slight waves. He is a well-put-together man, he dresses in a fitted suit with silk button-down shirts and Italian leather shoes. He has worked hard to be the man he is, or so he wants you to think, so he takes pride in how he looks. He usually has a slight stubble of facial hair, but a sharp haircut no matter what.

Why would he wear such an expensive suit for something like this? He is going to get it messed up in the tall grass. Oh well, not my problem, I mentally shrug to myself. Yes, the internet told me a lot about him, and previous customers have posted a lot of pictures for me to be able to get a look at not only his working side but also his more laid-back side and also of him dressed more like he is today.

James started his business R2R Construction, Rags 2 Riches, in 2010. Now, in 2015, he has 12 different crews of men, about 5-30 people per crew, that are constantly rotating from job to job keeping the sites on scheduled finish time. Budget seems to be the one thing that isn't discussed openly, probably because it can change at any given time. His company does everything from cement and framing work to electrical, HVAC, drywall, painting, finishing, and everything in between. I even saw he has a design team that consists of all women, which surprised me in itself.

"Hello, Ms. Dowes. I'm James Felden. I am so sorry I inconvenienced you by being a whole 2 minutes late. We better get started with viewing the property and house so I don't mess up your delicate schedule anymore." He snapped at me before reaching into his truck to grab a clipboard with the house schematics, and property line. I can almost feel his eyes roll even with his back to me.

I walk over looking at the clipboard, he smells like heaven and sin at the same time. I don't know his cologne, but it's intoxicating. "Where would you like to start?" I ask, smiling, trying to ease the tension I made.

He isn't amused, "I think the house is going to be the best bet since the outside and yard will be finishing touches and we can focus on that later when it is closer to being done." He seems cold, and I can tell he really isn't interested in being here.

I begin to lead him up the front stairs of the house, they are rickety and he makes sure to make a note of the porch as we make our way to the door. It creaks and is a little hard to open but it does, opening directly into the parlor/living room and we begin discussing the few things I want to change in this area. Once we have finished I lead him into the dining room on the right.

"I want to remove the wall between the dining room and the living room and kitchen. I know at least one if not both are going to be structural walls so I was thinking of an appropriate support beam from the era the house was built." I tell him as we stand in the dining room and I am pointing to the walls I am specifically thinking about.

He gives me a sidelong glance and I can feel the irritation coming from him like he didn't expect me to know anything about supporting walls so I just smile back at him.

With a raised eyebrow, he asked, "What do you think you might want to do with the kitchen since a large part of the cabinets would be gone with that section removed? Also, the stove is against the wall so you would need to know where it will go from there."

I can feel the way he says that like I am below him. Well he can fuck off. I know what will and won't work, he can suck it up and get used to me telling him how it will be.

I smile my most annoying girly smile and bat my eyelashes at him, "Well with that wall gone, I want to move the stove, since all the pipes in this house are so old they won't be up to code, it shouldn't be much of a problem to update it all and move it at the same time." I narrow my eyes at him as I say it, but I can feel his heated gaze on me and damn,

I now see why women swoon for him. He could make my panties wet just by looking at me, and he has!

He lets out a long annoyed breath, "I guess we can look at moving things but I don't think taking out the wall is an option."

"That's funny since I know it is a load-bearing wall, as long as you know how to properly reinforce the beam at the top, it will stand for another 200 years," I say as I saunter away, but I feel him watching me and the tension shifting. "Plus, I'm not saying remove it completely. I want an open floor plan so just a section has to be removed to open it all up." Grabbing some chalk I brought, I make an outline on the wall with a big X in the middle, turning back to face him, "I figured you might need a visual, so to help you," I point at the wall behind me now and smile, "This is the section I want to be removed, then a support beam at the top to pick up the load of what was removed. Does that make sense or do I need to help you with that too?" He wants to be an ass, I will show him how big of a bitchy brat I can be. While making notes on his clipboard, I head out of the dining area.

After he catches up to me in the kitchen, I finish saying, "I'm not just some girl that doesn't know anything about construction. You aren't going to be able to bully me, so you can stop acting like a misogynistic asshole. I don't know everything but I know enough and treat me like I'm an actual respectable client and person or I can find someone else." I'm staring at him like I could stab him if he says the wrong thing right now. "By the way, I am the lead designer for an architect company, I assist in all aspects of the build from beginning to end. I know what I am talking about. Don't treat me like I am beneath you, I'm your equal so get use to it"

He just stares at me not saying a word, jaw ticking, like he is imagining me just like that, beneath him, and good god I feel my panties becoming more wet.

How does he do that? How can he look at me with lust and disdain at the same time? I think to myself as I stand there and wait for him to respond.

I happen to quickly glance down once he lets out a long sigh, he is looking around the kitchen and making notes in his notebook, and he is hard. Good god the desire that shouldn't be building in me does just that. He never responded but I guess since he is taking notes, he has decided to back off for now.

"Would you like to move on or just stand around in the kitchen?" His tone caught me off guard, it's still rough but it's not filled with so much venom in each word.

Turning I lead him through the house, letting him look around and ask his questions while I explain what I want for each room. He writes down all my answers in detail before moving to the next room. We do this throughout the entire main floor adding a laundry area where the butlers pantry was. And the entire time he is cold and distant but the look in his eyes is piercing.

As we make our way to the second story of the house, I tell him about where I want the master bedroom, we walk through and talk about the walls we will have to tear out and build for the master bathroom.

He huffs at all my decisions, no matter how little. I think I hurt his ego and it makes me giggle to myself.

"Why do you want this room for your master bed and bath, the bedroom at the end of the hall would be better." He says with an exaggerated eye roll.

I just stare at him with annoyance dripping off me, "Because, the half bathroom that is downstairs is right below this room, which means when it is time to put in plumbing, it will be cheaper than running the pipes all over the house. Plus it's the original master bed and bath I want to keep size and we would only be taking a little from one of the other guest rooms. Why do you feel the need to undermine me at every turn?"

He is now looking at me like he could throw me out the window and walk away without thinking twice. I can feel his frustration but if I'm hiring him to remodel, he will learn to bend to what I want. It's not like I am asking him to do anything impossible.

"I just think you are going a little overboard. I mean all this costs money..." He starts to say but I'm not having it today. He already pissed me off.

So I decided to be a bitch, "Look here asshole, I get it. I am a woman and for some reason, you don't like working with women but if you are as good as they say, you're the one I want for this house. I am the customer, figure out an estimate and I will pay it in full before you start. Otherwise, note what you need, do as I ask as long as it is doable, and pull the stick out of your ass!"

I didn't mean to be that snappy but he pissed me off and I am done with him treating me like crap, but by the time I am done speaking, the fucker is smirking at me. WHAT THE HELL?

"Ms. Dowes, you're right. I guess I am being more of an asshole than needed. I will say you are the first woman I've worked around who has snapped at me like you do. It's cute. But I will watch myself, and you can help me too." His voice has shifted and it's almost sultry and the look in his eyes is pure lust.

Is he really flirting? No, I have to be imagining that. This guy can turn on a dime, this is going to be fun pushing his buttons. I narrow my eyes at him, letting out a sigh. I roll my eyes, turning and walking to the rest of the rooms explaining that all I want to do is update and get rid of one of the two bathrooms to put a Jack and Jill bathroom between the two bedrooms. But I keep catching him looking at my ass when he thinks I'm not paying attention. I push past him, literally shoulder-checking him, I hear a low growl but I walk back down the stairs like nothing happened.

After we finish the inside, we walk the grounds. I explained that the greenhouse is my personal project and I want it left alone. James gives me a side eye like he thinks I have no idea what I am doing but I explain that my dad and I used to build them around town when I was younger.

"I know what I want and how I want it. It will be my garden sanctuary so stay out." I say with more bite than intended but he just smiles and keeps walking. Maybe snapping at him actually did something.

It's nearing 5 pm by the time we are finishing the walk around. We end back at his truck.

"Ms. Dowes, I hope you understand that everything you want, though not unmanageable, is going to cost a lot. The house itself is going to need new studs, and new floor joists throughout to make it pass inspection along with new flooring throughout, and opening the main floor as much as possible is going to be VERY expensive in itself with support beams. I think, after walking around, we are looking at a starting budget of $2 million including the foundation and roof, but depending on what we find as we are working, it could be more or less." He tells me, almost expecting me to back down, he smirks at me. "If it is less, that money will just be transferred into the next step of renovations since we work in stages, but you will need to be available for approval if we run into issues, we will not proceed without your say"

I give him a curious grin, "That is actually less than I was budgeting for so it sounds like we have a good starting plan. Would you like me to bring the money to the office for your assistant in a couple of days? Also, I'll be staying 45 minutes away at my parent's house, but I will be here about everyday checking on progress. I will expect to be allowed on the property, with proper safety gear of course. I won't be coming inside unless escorted by you or someone on your team." I know that rubbed him the wrong way by the shift in his facial features, but he is arrogant and I like seeing him frustrated.

"Yes, just drop off the check with Alice in my office, I prefer a cashier's check or cash, she will give you a receipt for your records, once it is deposited we will be able to begin the demo. And as far as you on the job, that's a safety hazard and since you aren't OSHA certified I can't allow that. Insurance reasons and all, you understand." The look on his face tells me he thinks won. So I had to bust that bubble too.

Smirking as I let out a humorless laugh, "Oh, I am OSHA certified since I am an architect and all, and I tend to go to job sites, I have to be. So I will see you bright and early on the 21st." I full on smile at that because I know it grinds his gears by the sneer that spreads across his face as I turn and walk to my car.

"Please do not be in the way, especially with the demo crew. I honestly don't want you to accidentally get hurt. And I don't feel like dealing with the paperwork." He explains. I laughed out loud and that made him cock an eyebrow at me. "May I ask why that is funny?" He asks dryly as I open the door to my car.

"Fun fact, I know this isn't the military, but I was a Seabee, a construction worker, while I was on active duty in the Navy. I know safety and I know to stay out of the way. I won't be underfoot, you'll see when you all start." I say smiling as I slide into my car and shut the door.

I see him let out a big breath as he gets into his truck and turns around to leave. Thank god he is leaving before me, now I can breathe since I feel like I haven't since he got here.

The thoughts in my head are racing. He is massive and beyond sexy. I haven't thought about another man since Kenneth's death almost 2 years ago. James is invading my head and for the first time in what feels like forever, I am aroused to the point that I can feel my pulse in my clit just thinking about that impressive bulge in his pants when I mouthed off to him.

It's always the assholes that are most attractive. I remind myself and he is just that, an asshole.

I shake my head, trying to forget him and the scent of desire he left behind. He was an ass when I met him, but I guess I did start that. When the job starts I will make up for that and apologize when I come back. Depending on his mood that day at least. I smirk to myself before turning my car around and heading to my parents house.

James

What the hell just happened? I can't wrap my head around it! She is a little demon in a lamb suit and smells like sex that I could devour all fucking night. She makes all my blood drain to my cock but infuriates me at the same time. That smile as she was getting into her car, fuck me, all I wanted to do was bend her over the hood and fuck her till she was screaming my name.

I'm driving back to my office to drop off my notebook and the folder but my cock is throbbing thinking of her. I roll my shoulders trying to release some tension. Alice will still be there when I get there and I don't want to walk in with a raging hard on. I pride myself on control but Molly rips right through that without trying.

Looking in the rear view mirror, I still don't see her car behind me as I drive down the highway, so I chance it and pull off on the side of the road.

There is a gravel road just ahead and I decide to pull over there, it won't be as noticeable. I see cars passing by but I can't stop thinking about those perfect pink lips and what they would feel like wrapped around my cock. My balls hurt from want, I don't think I've ever hurt like this before.

As I come to a stop, I get a call from the office. Letting out a long breath, I answer.

"Alice, how can I help you?"

I can hear the smile in her voice, "Oh no, just calling to see how the meeting went."

As I listen to Alice, I feel my erection going down, she really is a good cock block right now, I smile because right now I needed that. "Well, she is definitely strong willed and infuriating, that's for sure. But as long as her check clears I guess I can tolerate her for that house."

Alice cackles at that, "It will be good for you. Plus that house will be worth it in the end. Does she want to do anything too modern for it?"

"Surprisingly no." I say with a little sigh of relief, for the house and my dick. "She wants to make the main floor a more open concept but that's the biggest modern move other than the obvious, updating the kitchen and bathrooms."

"Well then it sounds like your set. I am going home for the day, but I left a few messages on your desk. John from the Jackson site called and needed approval for something. Asked that you call him before lunch tomorrow. But other than that it's been quiet." She states politely.

"Alice, you really are a savior. Thank you for all your help. Have a good night and I will see you in the morning. I will be in at my usual time." I let her know with a smile and hangup.

Looking down, I'm no longer hard, which is good. Molly gets under my skin too much and I can't let this get out of hand. I have to keep my dick to myself on this one since she entices me too much. I don't need to fuck up what I have done here with a girl getting attached. I roll my neck and call Eric, he has been an employee since I started and the only person I talk to outside of Alice and customers.

As I put my truck into drive and turn around, Eric answers just as I am about to hang up.

"What's up fucker?" He is always so chipper when he answers my calls, it's annoying but I guess I'm the brodeing one.

"Oh you know, another day another dollar or some bullshit. Plans tonight?" I ask, knowing he doesn't. Unless he is working, neither of us do much of anything else but sometimes he goes on a date.

"You know I live a life of excitement, so no." He says laughing, "What are you thinking?"

"Let me run home and shower the day off," and the girl I just met at the site, "meet at Red Door? I need a beer." I say, knowing I will tell him more later but I don't want to over the phone.

"Sounds good, you ok though? You sound frustrated?" He asks bluntly, he is always curious. His brother committed suicide a couple years ago so he goes out of his way to make sure the men around him know they have someone to talk to if need be. It's honorable and I respect the hell out of him for it.

I laugh hard, "I will tell you in a bit. But overall I am good, thanks. I'll meet you there at 7."

Eric laughs also but agrees and we hang up.

As I am pulling into my drive, I realize I didn't go by the office. Oh well, it can wait till morning. I grab the files and put them under my seat to keep from prying eyes. They are sensitive but I don't want anyone seeing the name or address of my clients. I live in a safe neighborhood. Nothing special, nothing flashy and definitely nothing like I grew up in. The last thing I need to do is stand out. Being noticed would not have a good outcome for me. I don't need eyes on me or my family to find me. Let alone him. He might kill me, and I'm not sure how literal I am in that thinking.

The house I live in is a nice single story ranch style house. Three bedrooms and two bathrooms with a basement I turned into a media room. It's a neutral white and I painted the shutters and door black, mainly because it gave it a little face lift, but also because the nosey neighbor across from me said I couldn't. This isn't an HOA but she thinks she runs the area. So I did it partially to piss her off.

I pull up to the garage, before opening the doors, I check my surroundings. Nothing looks out of place. Same cars I see everyday, nothing new. Exactly how I like it. I have lived here since I moved to the area 5 years ago but I still check everything everyday. The minute I let my guard down, I know everything will go to hell.

I open my garage door and pull in, once the door is closed I get out of my truck and lock it before heading inside. I make my way through the kitchen, down the hall to my room. I decorated the whole place in all gray tones with black and white photos, it's calming to me.

Seeing different colors and the exaggerated lives that people like in their homes all day gives me a migraine, but this brings me peace.

I strip off my suit jacket and hang it up in the closet on the side for dry cleaning before stripping off my button down shirt and without realizing it, I get a whiff of Molly's perfume and I soak it in. It's subtle and smells like honeysuckle and freshwater. I can almost feel her body heat beside me again.

Shaking my head, *"No you can't go there! Stop thinking about her!"* I tell myself as I stride for the adjoining master bathroom. I strip my shoes, socks and belt as I start the shower. Leaning against the counter I take my pants off and fold them to add to the jacket and shirt for the cleaners.

I feel my heart rate pick up as the bulge in my boxer briefs grows. Molly is still in my head and I fucking hate it. I can't handle this right now. I try to ignore it as I take my briefs off and step into the shower.

Every time I close my eyes and take a deep breath, all I can think of is her. Her sweet scent, I would bet everything I have bet that she tastes as good as she smells. She has to be tight, she is so tiny, I couldn't imagine her being any other way.

Fuck it, I need a release. I grip the base of my cock and squeeze. Fuck me, just thinking about my hand being her tight cunt makes me groan. Slowly stroking myself, eyes closed I swear I can feel her gripping me, smell her arousal and I start pumping my hand harder and my hips faster. *"FUUUCK YES."* Growling at the image of her bent over in my head, I feel my body start to tingle and my balls draw tight as I come hard all over the shower floor. How the hell does the idea of her make me cum so fast, that isn't good at all.

Letting out a deep sigh of relief, I let myself relax for a moment before I start to wash.

Before long I am washed and in my closet for clean clothes. Jeans and a simple shirt since I am only having a drink with Eric. I will be lucky if he is out of his work clothes. I won't go out if I'm dirty, but Eric doesn't care, he could be covered in mud and he would still go to a nice place.

I finish getting around and head back to my truck. I have 30 minutes before Eric will call and see why I'm not there. He is a pain in my ass about being early everywhere he goes and it makes me laugh because looking at him you would think he is always late. I make my way to the restaurant knowing he should be getting there too.

Lone and behold, Eric is parked at the back of the parking lot looking at his phone when I pull in, asshole. I give him a half wavy as I park.

As I get out of my truck I hear him, "Hey man, on time for once."

I roll my eyes as I lock the truck up and shake his hand, "Look here fucker, I didn't have to ask you to come." I laugh out

"Okay okay. So what was going on earlier, you know you can talk to me, right?" I can feel his concern in the question.

"Let's get a drink and some food and I will explain how a demon dressed as a lamb fucked up my day." I explain as we make our way inside to the bar.

The place is packed, so we get a table on the bar side. I'm not overly interested in football but the Chiefs are a solid team to watch. Eric is a die hard fan though so he asks for a seat to watch whatever game is on at the moment.

As we eat and have a few drinks I explain my deal. Well all he needs to know at least.

"She's just a sassy little shit. I swear she is a demon but god damn she has the body of a fucking goddess." I tell him rolling my eyes as I take a drink of my beer.

Laughing so loud people look at him, "She got under your skin easier than I have ever seen. You never get this worked up over a hookup. We have worked together for 5 years and I have never heard of anyone getting to you like this. Hell I kind of want to meet her just to shake her hand" He bellows out.

"I swear renovating this house is going to be hell if she comes around everyday." I sigh at the thought.

"Well, why don't you just fuck her and get it out of your system? That always seems to work for you." He asks, raising his eyebrows. He knows that's what I usually do but something is different about her. I'm not sure if I like it.

"I just get the feeling she is going to cling, and I don't feel like dealing with that drama." I explain to him. It's not a lie but how do I say I want her without admitting I want more than just her pussy without sounding like a bitch

"Well, pick someone up tonight and get this chick out of your mind." He tells me, looking around like he is picking for me.

Just then, his eyes stick to the door, raising his eyebrows and I have to see what he is looking at. Turning around I pause before looking back to him and I can feel my face getting red but I'm not sure why.

"Fucking christ, that's her!" I almost slump in my chair like a child in trouble but his eyes are glued on her and I can feel my blood boil at the idea of him looking at her. I'm not usually possessive but with her I don't want anyone to watch her like I do.

His eyes light up, truly excited, "Man, if you aren't going to take her home then I will gladly take her off your hands." I can feel his excitement and I have never wanted to hit him so bad. I feel the anger rolling off me in waves.

I bare my teeth snarling at him, "You will NOT fucking touch her!"

Obviously shocked, he lifts his hands in surrender, "Okay, sorry man. Didn't mean to piss you off. You sure you don't want her, I've never seen you like this about pussy."

I roll my neck and apologies wiping my hand down my face, "See, I don't fucking know why but she fucking brought this out earlier and I am lost. I need to go home, here's my half." I pull my wallet out and slide some cash on the table, heading for the front door as Eric stares at me in pure disbelief. Hell, I can barely believe how I am acting.

Fucking hell, I see her out of the corner of my eye. She looks to be on a date and she looks fucking amazing. That lilac dress is hugging her in all the right ways. I feel my mouth drop open as I stare for a second.

I force myself to leave before I do something stupid as I see the guy she is with giving her a hug and his hand sets on the top of her ass and I see red. I barrel through the doors and to my truck. As I get in I punch the steering wheel, "WHAT THE ACTUAL FUCK DAM..." I cut that thought off before I finish it just in case someone who knows me hears and starts asking questions.

Pissed about Molly being on a date and about almost slipping up, I head home, where it is safe to be mad.

As I am pulling into my drive, I see my neighbor's sister outside. I need Molly out of my head, so this chick will do, although I don't usually do two nights in a row but I don't feel like going out anymore.

I invite her over, and decide I will fuck my frustration out before I lose anymore control.

5

Molly

I wake up Friday morning, calling my bank and informing them I need a check of $2 million for my renovations to be made out to Rags2Riches Construction. They informed me that it will take till Monday for them to clear that amount and to be pulled for such a large amount.

After I stretch and make my way from my room to the kitchen, my dad is sitting at the table drinking his coffee and reading the morning paper. I just stop and watch for a moment before he notices me, he reminds me of grandpa and I love it so much. When he notices me standing there he smiles and I notice the crows feet around his eyes, "Good morning sunshine."

I give him a warm smile as I walk over and give him a kiss on his cheek, "Good morning daddy. How did you and momma sleep?"

"Oh not bad, how did the walk through go with that contractor you were meeting? Oh and your date?" He asked, giving me a side look. He knows how hard it was for me to convince myself that it was ok to date again.

My dad is 63 and reminds me of my grandpa, so much. He has always been a great father and done everything he could to help support me. When I told him I bought the Quartan house he just laughed knowing that was the house I always dreamed of owning one day. It didn't help that he put in a word to the owners that I wanted it. He also adored Kenneth, so knowing I went on a date was a big step for me.

"Well, the contractor is going to be a pain in the ass, and before you ask, I can handle him. He just has to get it through his misogynistic head that I am the boss of my house, not him." I say with a laugh as

I roll my eyes at the thought of working with James Feldon on a daily basis and him getting mad over everything.

"You know I will help however I can but only if you want me to, but this is your house and your dream so I think it's good that you're taking control. And what about the date?" Giving me another long look, I see the curiosity written on his face. I think he is waiting for me to break down like I used to do when I thought about moving on. Now it feels, I don't know, kind of like the right time?

"That was ok. He was nice when he wasn't being domineering and he kept trying to take charge like I was a child. By the end of dinner I couldn't think of how to get out of there fast enough. So I made an excuse and went to get ice cream by myself before I came home." I gave him a look like I was disgusted. "I feel more comfortable about dating, I don't feel as much like I am cheating anymore and I know Kenneth would want me to move on, but it's still hard. But I figured I am moving on everywhere else in my life, I might as well work on moving on from him too. He can't come home but I feel like he would be disappointed if I didn't at least try." I don't know why but saying it out loud feels weird, and I shiver.

"Baby girl, you will know when the right person comes into your life. Be patient, you will never replace Kenneth, but you will find someone who will make you feel just as safe one day. They will accept that a part of you will always belong to Kenneth. Oh and I forgot to tell you, mom and I are taking off for a trip on Wednesday. We talked about it last night, and we are going to head up to Washington for a few weeks to see some old college friends." My dad is the sweetest, he always makes me feel hopeful and I am happy mom is feeling better so they are taking a trip. They have wanted this for so long, they deserve to do what they want.

"Good, you all should and I'll keep an eye on everything here till you get back." I say as I make some coffee. Turning to head out of the kitchen, "I am going to shower and head out to do some errands for the day. If you need anything just let me know before I leave or call me."

After I shower and get ready, I head over to Liberty to get some things done. Samples at Lowes, Hobby Lobby, lunch, maybe Target, never know what else.

As I get into Liberty, I head to Starbucks for a drink. Walking in, I see Jaz sitting in the corner working on her laptop. I get my drink ordered and walk over to say hi.

"Hey Jaz." I greet with a warm smile and couldn't help but admire her before I pulled her focus.

She seems deep in thought when she looks up, "Oh wow, hey Molly! How are you?" She beams like she is excited to see me. Which warms my heart, I don't talk to many of my high school friends, we seem to be in different parts of life anymore and I don't have much in common with them so it would be nice to make a new friend.

"I'm good, about to get ideas for the renovation. Try and make things between James and I run a little easier." I say as she is gesturing for me to sit with her, I'm rolling my eyes at the thought of him.

Jaz starts laughing, "Oh yes, James Feldon. I don't know him personally since I have only lived in the area for about 5 months but I heard he can be a pain to work with. You are definitely in for a treat from what I hear."

"That is one way to put it, we are like vinegar and water. We just don't seem to mix well but he is supposed to be the best, especially at older home remodels so I guess I will suck it up. Which is going to be funny because he doesn't like working with women from what I noticed so this is going to be fun. Plus for as much as he is an ass, he is nice eye candy so that helps a little." I sigh and slump in my chair a little.

"Oh I heard he is a looker too and a bit of a man-whore. I may have to come over to see how the work is going one day and try to sneak a look." She winks at me with a mischievous smile.

"Girl you don't have to sneak over, if you want to come with me one day I would be happy to take you over, but you will have to stay outside. I even promised I wouldn't go inside without an escort so no one gets hurt." I smile right back, knowing damn well it will piss James off.

"That would be great, I don't know anyone around here outside of work. Maybe we could get lunch when you're free also." I can feel the excitement in her tone.

Jaz seems so sweet and genuine, "That would be great. Since I moved home I don't talk to my old friends, it would be nice to have a new one. Plus you can help me make the hard decisions before I move in and we can have a wine and girls night at my house."

Jaz giggles with a reply, "Oh and you like wine. I think I found my new bestie."

My order is called so I turn to Jaz, "Call or text me whenever, I am always around. I'm an architect for a company here in the city but I am usually free to get together whenever. I luckily work from home." I write my number on a piece of paper and give it to her. "I am going to get out of your hair. Hope you have a good day."

"Have a good day and I will text you in a bit so you have my number too." Jaz tells me as she stands and gives me a hug.

Yeah, she is definitely going to be my new best friend.

After I get my chai tea latte and wave bye to Jaz, I head to Lowes to get some ideas. I know it will make it easier if I have my ideas in order now and James can't argue about it not being done later.

Once I get to Lowes, I start walking around to different areas, getting samples and taking pictures of items and adding notes in my phone with the names of different things. I am walking through the paint aisle making my way to flooring, not paying attention, when I walk right into a wall of a man.

I huff out a breath, but I don't have to look up to know who I literally ran into. He smells of cedar and whiskey and it's just as intoxicating as yesterday. I try to refrain from rolling my eyes and look up at him, only to see him smirking at me already.

"Good morning Ms. Dowes." Is all James says and I am not sure if he is being nice or not. I feel the tension rolling off him but unlike yesterday, he isn't in a suit. He has on work boots, an old stained pair of jeans and a stained t-shirt with a few holes in it. I can't help but stare as I feel the saliva building in my mouth. He really is a gorgeous man to look at.

Swallowing, I look at his perfectly chiseled jaw with a slight stubble, a mischievous smirk plastered on his face, and his eyes are blazing.

"Morning. I didn't mean to hit you, I was looking at paint samples." I state the obvious with a smart ass tone and a small eye roll.

"I noticed that, don't you think it's far too early for you to be picking paint, since you haven't even paid me to start working on the house yet?" lifting an eyebrow, he just stares back at me but I can see he is still slightly smiling.

I shift on my feet, "I already called the bank and I picked up the check Monday morning so I will be dropping that off before 11 am. When it comes to paint, I may not be an interior designer but I want to have everything picked before you get to that point to make sure we have it ordered and ready so there aren't any hold ups. I already told you, I'm not an idiot and I know how to plan accordingly."

James lets out a soft laugh, "Okay Ms. Dowes, may I call you Molly? Seems like I'm going to be seeing you a lot and it would be nice to be a little more casual."

I keep my guard up, something seems off but not in a bad way and I can't put my finger on it, but I relax a little as I tell him, " Yes, Molly is fine and yes you will be seeing me a lot." I can't help but feel the tingle that runs through my entire body under his gaze. My core is tight and as much as I want to say he isn't the reason, I know better.

His smile is almost feral as he replies, "Wonderful Molly. You aren't wrong about having everything picked before hand and it adds up fast but when you're sure you know what you want, bring it to me or drop it off at my office and I will get the appropriate amount ordered for you and possibly be able to find the same product somewhere else for less, save you a little money. I have a warehouse of storage units that I keep my customers' stuff in for the jobs so it will be safe there till I need it." He adds with a wink, "I would be happy to help you if you would like also."

"I appreciate the offer but I am just getting ideas to take home and work out what I want. I'll let you know when I am ready, thank you. But I know you're a busy man, I won't keep you any longer. Have a good day." I say as I side step him and start towards the flooring area.

He doesn't say anything but I can feel his eyes on me, before I realize it, he is walking up beside me. Still not saying anything yet, I feel him looking at me out of the corner of his eye, "So, how was your date? I saw you at the Red Door as I was leaving last night." he says matter of factly.

I stumble at his words, "Oh, yeah, it was, umm…" I trail off, not sure how to answer that. It feels personal but I don't know him well enough to be honest, but he saw me so I guess it is ok but before I can finish what I was saying, James grabs my wrist and turns me to him.

"Did he hurt you? Are you ok?" He says as he brings me to a halt, looking at me like he is searching for injuries.

I cock my eyebrows and my mouth drops open before saying, "Oh god no nothing like that. We just didn't seem to click." I am still staring at him lost by his concern.

Where did that come from? First he is cold and belittling, then he is acting like he is a starving man and I am the only meal he has seen in a month, and now he seems concerned for me. This man is going to give me whiplash with his mood swings.

Out of nowhere, I see a mask of the original stern man slide back across his face, "Sorry, it's none of my business. I have to go, have a good day." He states as he lets go of me and turns to almost run away.

What the fuck was that about?

I am left standing there reeling before I shake my head and go to the flooring section, trying to get that whiplash to leave my mind.

Before I realize it, it is lunch time and I have spent all morning getting samples and ideas from Lowes. As I am leaving to head to my car to find lunch, I get a text from Jaz and I save her number.

"Hey girl, it's Jaz. My lunch date just canceled and I was wondering if you wanted to join me? I hate eating alone." She adds a laughing emoji.

"Yeah, I was actually about to find lunch anyways. Where do you want to meet?" I send back to her.

"Honestly I was just thinking something like Panera, how does that sound?"

"Yeah that sounds perfect. I will head there now, I'm only about 3 minutes away. See you soon." With that I am in my car, when I notice James' truck is parked right in front of my car. I know it's his because I look in the cab and he is sitting there, glaring at me.

Again the whiplash again. What is his deal?

I smile and wave as I get into my car and back out. Heading to Panera to find Jaz which is only at the other end of the parking lot. She is already inside waiting for me as I park, so we order our food and find a place to sit and wait for our food.

I look out the window in time to see James driving by, I think at least, it looks like his truck again. Maybe I am going crazy, he isn't stalking me or anything crazy like that. The glare he gave me as I was leaving Lowes got under my skin, there is definitely tension there but I'm not sure if it is my sexual tension or his brooding tension.

I roll my neck and focus on lunch with Jaz. We laugh and have a nice time, she is easy to fall into conversation with. We spend the next hour and half chatting and getting to know each other before she has to get back to work.

Heading to my car to go home and print off pictures to organize things. My parents are leaving soon and I'll help them get packed and ready. I also make sure I head by the bank, they don't need extra money but they helped me my entire life, I'll help them now, so I pull out $5000.

When I get home, I go to my mom and give her the money, telling her if they need it, they have it and if they need more to just tell me and I will deposit it into their account. I know if I try and give it to my dad he won't take it, stubborn jerk, guess I know where I get it from. I smirk and my mom knows what I am thinking without me saying a word.

After I kiss my mom on the forehead, I head to my room to start printing pictures and seeing how I like colors, flooring, counters, and all the in-betweens together. Before I realize it, it's dinner and I spend the rest of the evening helping my parents before we all head to bed.

In my room, changing for bed, I get an eerie feeling like I am being watched, but we live in the country and no one comes out here. I guess James's glare got under my skin more than I thought. But the heat in his eyes is what keeps me looking around my room as I crawl into bed.

I am exhausted, but as I close my eyes, I feel movement outside my window and I bolt over to look out. Damn cat runs by, lord knows what he is chasing now. So I roll my eyes and go back to bed. Before long, my eyes are falling shut and I am fast asleep.

6

James

Monday morning rolls around, after following Molly home Friday, I couldn't help but look in her window, catching her as she was getting ready for bed only made me want her more. Fuck she has the body of a goddess, but she is fire and the closer I get, I can feel I'm going to get burned. Something in me calls to her, and I haven't felt that since my father made my high school sweetheart disappear 6 years ago. He said she was a distraction. I still don't know exactly what he did, knowing him, she is at the bottom of a river or he married her to a family back in Ireland.

I shake the memories clear out of my head, *I left, no need to keep letting my mind wander back.* I just have to keep reminding myself.

I avoided Molly's house the rest of the weekend, and her to be honest. I don't need to catch feelings and something about her makes feelings come to the surface I didn't realize I still had. She's innocent, and I am a wolf that will rip her to shreds and smile at my victory.

I get around and head to the office. It's only 4:30 in the morning and Alice called and said she wasn't feeling good so I told her to stay home and get rest. I will go check on her later this afternoon.

I head towards the office, stopping by Starbucks since coffee won't be ready when I get there. I ordered an iced chai tea latte, the same that Molly ordered Friday. Why? I don't know, since I would usually get a venti black coffee, no sugar, no cream. For some reason I want to try what she likes.

As I get into the office, I start the coffee pot so I have more, and head into my office leaving the door open so I can hear if anyone comes in. I sit back at my desk, drinking the latte I got. I can see why she likes it, it has a good flavor and it's not too sweet.

Before I realize it, my morning has flown by and I glance at the clock on my desk and see it's nearly 11 am when I hear the door open. Standing from my chair, I am in jeans and a t-shirt since I have to visit a jobsite. I start for the front, "Good morning, how can I help you today?" I try to say as nicely as possible, since I'm not usually the one to greet people.

Just as I finish my sentence, I round the corner to Molly standing there looking so fucking delicious. Fuck me, I forgot she said she was coming by today.

She's wearing a pair of jeans that hug her body perfectly, and a semi-tight shirt tucked into her pants with brown knee high boots. I could easily bend her over and devour her till she is putty in my hands, literally. I can feel myself smirking, when I fix my face.

What's my deal with the idea of bending her over? I roll my neck to regain control.

She raises an eyebrow at me, "Hi, I didn't expect you to be here." She steps toward me and it takes everything in me to distract myself so she doesn't notice the bugle in my jeans that I can feel growing just by having her near. I pull my shirt down, like I am smoothing it out, and also step forward before she finishes her statement. "As promised, here is your cashier's check from the bank to start renovations on my house." She has a smirk on her face and I won't lie, I want to grab her and see if those lips are as soft as they look.

"Wonderful, I will deposit today. Thank you" Is all I can say. I have to watch myself so I don't do something stupid. She seems to linger though so I go on. "Did you have a nice weekend?" I ask, moving around to Alice's desk so I can pull out a deposit form and fill it out.

I hear her voice, soft, almost timid, which is odd for her, "Oh, it was ok, my parents left early for a trip to Washington, so I helped them pack and get on the road."

For the love of god, she looks so innocent right now. If she knew I was outside her house Friday night, she wouldn't be telling me her parents left early, hell she wouldn't be hiring me.

"Oh, that will be nice." I can manage to say. "Well I am going to deposit this, is there anything else you need?" I ask to keep this professional.

"Maybe a receipt from you validating that I dropped it off. I keep meticulous records of my finances." She gives me a look like I should have known.

"Of course, my apologies. Alice is the one that usually does all this for me so I forget when she is out." I shrug it off as that and not the fact that I can't think straight around her.

As I write the receipt and rip it out of the book, she is quieter than I would expect. It's almost off putting since she has been so open about her thoughts up to this point. I offer a tight smile as I hand it to her, "Here you are. Is there anything else?" I feel like she wants to say something but those doe eyes are searing into my soul and I can feel the heat.

"No, thanks. Have a good day." She says as she turns to leave.

I hear her get into her car and leave before I move from behind the desk. My cock didn't get the message that we can't go there and he likes to be seen when she comes around. I palm myself as I walk back into my office.

I can't go there, but fuck me I need a release, Jane from Thursday didn't do it for me at all. Ever since I met Molly, she is the only woman that fills my mind. Why has she gotten into my head? Maybe it's because she is strong willed and isn't afraid to stand up against me. I'm not used to women not backing down when I talk, and Molly definitely fights that.

I am going to have to put a damper on my dick somehow and find a way to be more of an ass to her or just keep avoiding her. I can't keep allowing this to happen, I can't let her keep getting to me like she does.

She could be my undoing if I let her rip the control I keep on myself. I know she doesn't know it or how bad it could be but it would be dangerous for me and her both.

Watching her Friday night through her window was pushing it, but at least I'm not touching her, right? I wanted to crawl in her window while she was sleeping and spread her legs wide just to eat her pussy as she was writhing and clawing at my head screaming through an orgasm.

Fuck, just thinking about it makes my cock throb against my zipper begging for a release. I can't imagine what would happen if I actually got my hands and tongue on her. I palm my cock, a low growl comes from deep in my chest at the pressure. Thinking about Molly coming back and me forcing her to her knees as she opens her mouth and begs me to throat fuck her. Fuck me the idea in my head is making my heart rate go up.

I shift in my chair, turning to where my back is to the door, just in case.

Unzipping my jeans, and moving them and my briefs out of the way, releasing my cock. I groan at the relief and see pre-come already glistening the tip, gripping my cock hard at the base, I stroke myself, moaning and thrusting into my hand.

"FUCK" I growl. All I can think about is Molly's soft lips wrapped around me.

Before I realize it, my muscles are tensing and I am coming all over my stomach, growling her name. "Fuck Molly"

I sit there letting myself relax for a moment before I get up. I feel like a teenager who has never seen a pussy before. The thought of her makes me come harder and faster than I ever have in my life and it almost pisses me off. If I ever fucked her, I would fuck that up and she would think I am a one pump chump, probably laugh me out of this town.

I lean over and grab a tissue to clean myself up and I already feel more relaxed. Like I can breathe again. After I clean up, I get to work, clear headed finally or at least for a little while.

The rest of the afternoon went smoothly. I deposited Molly's check, set up everything to start the gutting on her house, and headed to a couple job sites to check on progress.

7

Molly

I dropped off the check with James and I swear I could feel sexual tension, and god it's driving me nuts. I haven't wanted someone since Kenneth, and I know I should move on but James is mysterious, dark and I feel something dangerous about him. I feel it in my gut but I can't put a finger on it. I happened to glance at the bulge he was trying to hide, and fuck me, what I wouldn't give to see that in all its glory.

I decide I am going to look into him more though, on a more personal level. So I head to Starbucks, because why not drink my lattes while I do so.

Settling at a table in a corner so my laptop is hidden to anyone who comes in. I get my iced chai latte and start googling James Feldon.

Google immediately brings up everything I know. He's a handsome, rich 35 year old man, who started his business 5 years ago. Other than that, there's nothing about him, it's like he didn't exist. There are NO records of him being born, where he grew up, his family, high school or college. He just appeared. That is all too suspicious and I don't like it.

"That's impossible" I mutter to myself. I was so engulfed in research, I didn't see Jaz come in.

She sits beside me before I realize she is here, "What's impossible?" She whispers while nudging me in the ribs.

I slam my laptop shut blushing but it's too late, she saw what I was doing and I have been caught red handed.

"Oh, why are you looking into James? Did something happen over the weekend? I seen you yesterday but you didn't mention anything." She drills me with questions.

"No, nothing happened. I just have a weird feeling about him and I'm not sure if it's good or bad, but I know he is hiding something. I feel it in my gut and I can't figure out what it is." I tell her, rolling my eyes and sighing.

Something is off with him, and I am determined to know what it is. I remind myself.

Jaz laughs, "I think you are interested in him and it just scares you. After everything you went through with Kenneth, I think you're reserved, which is totally understandable. But James is just private. Everyone I know that has worked with him says he values his privacy more than anything."

I sigh and sit back in my seat, "I don't think that's it. I just feel like there is more." Opening my laptop I showed her what I was looking at. "Before 5 years ago he didn't exist. But 5 years ago, James Feldon appeared. But not a thing before then. You can't just appear, there would be something but with him, there is literally nothing."

"Molly, look at me." I slowly turn and look at her. "You're under a lot of stress, you just made 2 huge purchases in less than a week, which is stressful on anyone. But you are letting the stress get to you. You need to relax, I think you are letting all this work you up too much." She holds my hands gently. I can see the concern in her face.

I take a deep breath, and slump a little. "Maybe you're right, I need to unwind. Maybe I just need to get laid and that is why I am so wound up." I fake a laugh but Jaz sees right through it.

Jaz smiles faintly, "I don't have anything to do today, I'll call into the office and let them know I won't be there and we'll have a girls day. A client gave me and a friend a day pass to her spa, so I'll call and see if we can get in." she pulls out her phone before I can answer.

A few moments later, she turns to me smiling like a crazy person. "Ok, she said if we can be there in the next 30 minutes, she has plenty of time to get us in."

I smile and let out a sigh, she is probably right anyways, shutting my laptop and stuffing it in my purse. "You're right, let's go and then after we can get wine and head back to my house and have a wineaholics night" I say laughing. She is laughing as she takes my arm in hers and we wander out the door.

"How about we take one car. If you want to drive I will leave my car at Target till we come back through." she suggested.

"That sounds perfect. And we can't forget dinner when we get wine, I love my food too much to forget about that. I have to have food, since my parents left yesterday morning, I still haven't gone shopping." They weren't supposed to leave till Wednesday but they were excited and wanted to go so I helped them get on the road early.

After we drop off her car, we make our way to the spa. The place was nice and the more I was there getting a massage and mud bath, I think she was right. I changed a lot in my life in one week and maybe the stress was weighing on me more than I thought.

After the spa, we go back to her car, I go for wine and she goes for food. An hour later, we are meeting at my parent's house giggling like old friends as we make our way inside, hands filled with more food and wine than two people need. We take everything to the kitchen, laying the food out like a buffet.

After we make our plates and grab wine, a bottle each, we go to the living room to pick a show and have a girls night giggling and talking.

Jaz is passed out on the couch after 3 bottles of wine to herself. I smile and cover her with a blanket, taking a moment to admire her beauty again. I have never been with a woman, but she is sexy and I would be interested in trying. I shake my head and then head to take a shower.

All clean and feeling more relaxed than ever. With a towel wrapped around me, I leave the bathroom to go to my room to get clothes but I gasp and stop dead in my tracks when I enter.

James, he is in my bedroom. How? He is staring at me like he is about to murder me.

"W-what?" I stumble on my words. "How did you get in here?" I ask softly and I can hear my voice shaking.

He doesn't say anything, he just stares and I can see his chest heaving with each breath. I feel like he can see me through my towel. I feel naked under his intense stare and technically I am under the towel.

He stalks toward me and my feet are cemented to the floor and he gently tugs my towel free. I don't fight for some reason though. I let him take it and just that alone confuses me more.

In this moment, as he is staring at me his gaze consumes me and every thought in my head. I hear sirens in the distance from town about a mile away, the cool spring breeze coming from the open window directly behind him gives me goosebumps, the natural hardwood floors are chilly on my feet and as he stares at my naked body, I feel like I am the most important yet most exposed thing in this house. He reaches out and gently touches my cheek, letting his finger glide from my cheek, down my neck, onto my shoulder and slowly caressing my full breast which feels much more heavy than usual. His touch is intoxicating and I can't help but lean into it.

He is an intimidating man, but I can see the compassion that he hides behind walls. His touch is gentle but firm and I shake as I am feeling his fingers move across my skin. Goose bumps covering my body.

I have never been this aroused by a man just standing in front of me barely touching me. He's wearing jeans and a t-shirt from earlier today. Everything hugs his muscles as if, if he turns too fast, his clothes will rip into pieces. He bends over and licks the already hard peak of my nipple making me almost collapse with the electricity he sends through my body and I let out the breath I didn't know I was holding.

He shifts a little closer before sliding his hand down my stomach and slowly around to grab my ass. His fingers gently glide between my legs. I feel the tip of his middle finger brush against the tight entrance of my ass and then slowly he moves to my slit. Already moist with anticipation, I let out a small gasp as I lean into him, almost begging for his fingers to enter me. He begins to gently rub my clit and I can feel my body rubbing against his hand and I let out a soft moan and melt into his touch.

In that moment, James stands straight, steps back and shakes his head like he is confused. "I shouldn't be here, it's wrong, I'm sorry!" James snaps. He pushes past me, almost running out of my room. I hear his footsteps as he moves quickly through the house and slams the door as he leaves.

I am still standing there stunned, and naked. My body is still tingling from his touch when I let out a sigh.

What the hell was that? Why? How did he even get in?

Then the realization of the open window sets in, he must have climbed through it.

I have a million questions running through my head but it's all confused with how he just touched me. Like I was something special, or more. My curiosity quickly turns to anger and I can feel my blood start to boil.

He is an asshole! I really can't stand how he always thinks he is better than everyone. He is also gorgeous and mesmerizing to every woman around here, including me, but I refuse to give him the satisfaction of showing him how much I want him. I swear his ego gets bigger every time a woman eye fucks him in public. Then I remember his hands on me and I would give anything to feel that again.

Fuck me! What's wrong with me?!

I put my towel back on and check on Jaz, but she didn't even notice the door slamming and I sigh in relief. I mean I will tell her tomorrow but tonight, what the fuck just happened? I don't even know, so how am I supposed to explain it to her right now?

8

James

What the fuck was I thinking! That was stupid and impulsive! I have to keep my distance. But I can't resist her! Her body calls to me and I can't help it.

I drive home pissed at myself, but I still smell her sweet scent on my fingers. She was so tight and fuck she was wet, and not from her shower. I wanted to pin her to the wall and taste that tight, sweet cunt. I didn't want just my fingers touching her. I wanted to pull my cock out, pick her up and slide my dick so deep in her she wouldn't be able to walk right. I want to see those perfect tits bounce and feel the way her cunt strangles me as an orgasm rips through her.

"FUCK" These damn clothes are too much! They feel like they are trying to strangle me all over. Pulling on the neck of my shirt I can feel the breath leave me shakily. I need to get home and get this shit off before I have a panic attack. I should have just gone home after work, not by her house, I knew better!. "That was a mistake!" I'm yelling at myself.

Once I get home, I rush inside, stripping off my clothes with every step I take letting them stay wherever they fall. I go straight to my bathroom to turn on a cold shower. I need to wash her smell off my fingers, but I don't want to at the same time. I want to jerk off to her scent. Seeing her this afternoon made me horny, but smelling her sweet arousal on me makes me feral to my core.

Even her cunt smells like heaven, just on my fingers I can smell how she smells like she was made for me, like her soul calls to mine. She is my own drug, and I'm fucking addicted to her. I'm an addict, but I have to get clean. I can feel it in my bones she is the one drug I can't have or it will kill me or worse her.

53

I make myself get into the ice-cold shower, I have to make this raging hard-on go down. I start thinking of nursing homes, the elderly, anything that will help make this go down so I can sleep this night off. Nothing is working though, so I turn the water to hot and I let it beat down on me as I wrap my hand around my cock and brace myself against the wall. I'm almost frantic at this point.

I smell her on my fingers and stroke myself faster, closing my eyes and letting the smell of her consume my thoughts. I need to feel her, taste her, devour her. I need to fill her completely with my come and watch as it leaks out of her then crawl between her legs and eat both of our orgasms out of her till she is coming on my face and sated. Pumping faster, I can feel my legs shaking with the need building in me.

At that thought, I grip my cock so tight, stroking and coming so hard that I lose my footing for a moment and my come paints the shower wall in a thick ribbon.

Fuck me I haven't come that hard since... No, I can't think about that, I shake the thoughts off. Molly is now and I need her but I shouldn't.

After I clean myself up, I scrub the shower before stepping out and getting ready for bed. Letting the memories of the past fill me, remembering why I shouldn't involve Molly in my life. I shouldn't let anyone get close to me, it's the only way to keep them safe. I won't end up like my father and Molly is too perfect to be caught in this web. I shouldn't trap her in my secrets. It's the best way to keep her safe.

But I'm not a good enough man to walk away, and I can't let a woman that perfect go. Letting all that settle into the back of my mind, I settle into bed and let the rest of the night fade away.

I work the rest of the week, staying busy and not allowing myself to go to Molly's house in the evening. I'm working till I am ready to pass out. I've also been avoiding Eric, I don't feel like telling him how I fucked up. I know he won't see it as big of a fuck up, but he also doen't know me as well as he thinks he does.

Saturday I decide I'm going to take off to my favorite kitchen and bath warehouse in Olathe. I know Molly was already looking but I get a good deal here so I will get a catalog and show her better options than Lowes, even if it's just the price difference I get. Plus this keeps me busy so I know I won't be tempted to try and see her.

My phone has been on silent when I haven't been at work so when I turn it on, I see a missed call from Eric and a voicemail. He knows I will get back to him when I'm not busy so he doesn't keep bothering me unless it's an emergency but I decide to go ahead and listen to the message.

"Hey James, you must be busy if you're turning your phone off or on silent, but I saw you on the site so I know you're ok. I just wanted to give you a heads up, I was at Starbucks on Monday and I saw your girl," I smile at myself because I wish I could say she was mine. "I didn't hear the whole conversation but she was with a friend and, because they were almost whispering, I heard her saying something to her friend about you and then they were looking at her laptop. They both looked a little puzzled and then something was said about just appearing. I don't know, I doubt it is anything or even about you but it felt off and I figured I'd mention it. Hit me up when you're ready to stop being a brooding dick. Later."

By the end of the message, I have a mixture of feelings. Was she looking into me? Why? What did she find or not find? What is she questioning?

I feel the anger boiling in my veins and I have to figure out what she is doing. So I quickly came up with a plan.

It's Friday evening, and I am hidden in the woods around Molly's parents house. I left my truck in a field about a mile away that I hunt at so I know it's hidden from sight also.

Molly comes out the front door on her phone, "Yea, I am leaving now. I double checked that I have everything so I will be there in 30 minutes. You better not be too far ahead of me, you owe me at least five drinks already." She giggles and fuck if that sound alone doesn't make my balls pull tight and my cock throb.

She gets into her car and leaves.

I wait another 15 minutes in the woods to be sure the coast is clear before I walk up to her house and walk right in. I saw she didn't lock it and I plan to punish her for that later. Tonight I'm placing cameras to keep a better eye on her.

I put four hidden cameras in the living room, ensuring one is pointed at the door, before I head into the kitchen and place three more. I'm making sure on my phone I can see all angles and hear everything before I move on. Staring at the bathroom I contemplate it, but I think that is a little too pervy, even for me. I may not be the good guy everyone assumes I am but I'm not that bad. Shaking my head and turning to the next room.

I move into her bedroom and stop. It smells like her and my cock reminds me that I can't get off enough to her but I ignore that urge for now. Placing far more cameras than necessary all over her room, including the footboard of her bed, in my defense I don't know where she sits when she is on her computer, at least that's the lie I'm telling myself. She has a desk in her room that she obviously uses. Her charger is even at her desk so that has to be where she uses it most.

I check my phone to make sure I can see where I want, including the foot of her bed since I put a camera on each corner of her foot board.

Ok, maybe I am that pervy. I think so myself and roll my eyes, shrugging to myself. I want to see if she fucks herself thinking of me or says my name as she orgasms like I do with her. I want to see if I can see that tight pussy, even a glimpse might help my curious mind.

As I turn, I see her dirty clothes basket and I know I shouldn't, I go through till I find the panties closest to the top. When I got here I heard the shower on from outside, she must have worn these today as I lifted them into the moonlight and holy hell they are still moist. My half hooded eyes and my throbbing cock tell me to take them and I will but I want to smell her again so I pull them to my nose and inhale. I can feel the scent of her taking over my core and my semi-hard cock is now full hard and aching like never before.

I can feel the precum leak from my cock and I smile. The panties smell like her arousal and are so wet, she must have gotten off wearing them. So I do what any rational man in my position would do, I go to the kitchen and find a Ziplock bag, seal them in and pat my cock, "soon" I tell it as I put the panties in my pocket and head out to leave.

Before I make it to the door, I see the bag she usually carries. I have only been here about 30 minutes and if she goes out tonight, I have time to snoop a little more before she will be home.

I open the bag and immediately see her laptop so I pull it out and open it. It isn't password protected. *She really needs to protect herself better.* I think to myself as I shake my head. Once it is open, I see what I was looking for without searching, it's right there on the homepage and fire blows through my blood. A folder, 'James Feldon' so I open it and there are notes, pictures, website articles and a subfolder named background check. I open the notes first and see she has a lot of questions. Like who is he? James Feldon or someone else? Is he running? Is he dangerous? Where is he from? Witness protection?

The last one makes me smirk but I'm still pissed she is looking into me but she hasn't found anything, not yet at least. The guy that gave me a new identity was decent but not great. Finding a great one to get papers from would have alerted the wrong people.

I close the notes and open the background check and instantly see red, I have to sit down. I'm so livid I can't stop shaking. It's a copy of an original document with a handwritten letter.

'Hey Mols, I did the favor you asked, just know if anyone asks I didn't. This is everything I found on this James Feldon guy. All I know is he is a ghost. He didn't exist before 5 years ago, like at all. I don't know who he really is, there is nothing in any of the FBI documents about him or an alliance that connects to this name. Be careful, I don't know how dangerous this guy is or isn't. He may have just needed a fresh start or it could be something a lot more serious. Watch yourself, remember even the devil was once an angel.

P.S. Do NOT ask a favor of that caliper from me again. I could lose everything.

B'

Who the fuck is B? Why are they looking into the FBI database? This is getting too close! At least they didn't find my real name anywhere but I have to put an end to this somehow.

I close the programs I opened, shut the laptop and put it back where I found it and leave before I let my anger get the best of me.

9

Molly

Jaz and I stayed out much later than we expected for a Saturday night, but we had fun and I think we both needed it. A little too much, so we had to have an Uber take us back to my place, I left my car at the bar. We'll come back for it somehow tomorrow, when I'm not drunk and I care.

By the time the Uber gets us back to my house we're laughing like mad women and leaning all over the other for stability. I pay the driver and as I am backing out of the car Jaz is waiting for me to go inside. I hook her arm in mine and we stumble our way through the door, tripping over each other and giggling as I fall on top of her on the floor.

Staring at her mouth for a moment too long, and feeling awkward I roll over, "I'm so sorry, damn drunk feet..." Is all I get out before Jaz wraps her hand around the back of my neck and pulls me to her for a kiss.

Shock hits me first but then I let the desire take over and kiss her back. Her lips are like silk and her tongue touches my mouth for entrance. I let the moment happen and fully kiss her, our tongues tangle but the kiss is gentle and not rushed. I can definitely feel more than just a kiss between us.

Pulling away after a moment, "I-I'm sorry, I shouldn't have assumed," Jaz says breathlessly, her cheeks flush and she starts to push away. I grab her wrist and stand with her.

"Don't be sorry, I wasn't sure about any of it, so I never tried first but I wanted to all night." I can feel the blush in my cheeks but I don't look away. I feel comfortable telling her and not be embarrassed.

"Hold on, so it wasn't just me then?" The question holds heat in her eyes.

"No, I didn't know if you liked me like that and I've never been with women so I didn't know how to approach it." I can feel the relief in my tone.

Jaz laughs and it makes me giggle with her. "How about we go back to our normal night and we can discuss more about the kiss when we are sober."

I let out a sigh, "You know, that is probably a good idea, well sort of."

"What does sort of mean?" she says, cocking an eyebrow at me.

I hook my arm through hers to pull her to the kitchen, "Well I won't lie, that was... nice, and if you'll let me I will probably do it again." I say with my back to her as I am getting some water from the fridge.

"Oh, well I would be ok with that, but I do want to talk more about James, and I also know that man would be the best ride of either of our lives." I've noticed she is easily distracted when she is drunk and it's so cute.

Rolling my eyes I walk into my bedroom, unzipping my dress as I go, Jaz is following close behind.

"I am sure he would and I would be lying if I said I haven't thought about him when I play with myself. There is also something else though, it's sexy as hell but I don't know if it can be trusted. Like is he bad boy/fuck toy or is he bad boy/slit your throat." I laugh as I fall on my bed trying to get my heels off. I'm only being half sarcastic.

Finally stripped, I pull out pajamas for us both and hand some to her.

"You know you could just ask him, didn't you say he is starting demo on your house Monday?" She questions.

"Yes but have you ever tried to talk to him, let alone seen him in person? He's not an easy man to just be like 'oh hey buddy, what are you hiding? I can't find anything about you and it makes me wonder if you are a serial killer." I don't hide the sarcastic tone this time. Jaz is laughing at me and it makes me laugh also.

After we are dressed, we make our way back to the living room but Jaz sees me looking around.

"What's wrong?" cocking her head to the side, looking in the same direction I am.

"Um, I don't know," I say as my brows furrow and I keep looking around my room. "Something feels off but nothing is." I shake my head and head towards her, "It has to just be all the shots you forced me to drink." I say as I laugh and follow her to the living room.

Once we settle on the couch I start showing her what I have on James. Yes I may be stalking a little bit but my gut is rarely wrong and my gut says he is hiding something.

As Jaz is reading through the little bit of information I have, I am looking for something on TV for background noise.

"Who is B?" Jaz asks.

"Oh, yea that's a friend from where I was stationed. I promised I wouldn't tell anyone who they are, so as much as I trust you, I have to respect that." I give her a pinched smile because I don't NOT want to tell her but, what they did could get them fired.

She smiles at me, "And you keep getting better and better." She leans over and kisses my cheek and I blush like a little kid. But as she laughs again as she turns and leans back on the other side of the couch, "So you actually like him. I mean you're going through a lot of trouble to find out so much about him so I assume you like him." She doesn't sound jealous when she says it and it makes whatever this is with her and I better.

"Really! Have you seen him? And somehow he makes my body light up and my core heat. I just want to trust him. I'm under no illusion that he is a 'good guy' but I do want to know more. And..." I trail off, knowing I haven't told her about last weekend yet.

"Oh no! you can't say 'and' and just stop! Spill it!" She jolts up to sit straight up and stares at me with a devilish smile waiting for the latest gossip.

"Well last weekend when we had our girls night and you passed out on the couch," I raise an eyebrow and smirk back at her. "Well I showered and when I went into my room to get clothes after, James was in there. Just standing there staring at me." I paused for a moment before continuing, "He took my towel off, and just touched me and maybe slightly fingered me but out of nowhere he backed away like he was waking up. It was like he was mad and he stormed out. Honestly, I'm surprised he didn't wake you up by how hard he slammed the door behind him." I can't tell if I'm embarrassed or still mad at him for that.

Her smile has left her face and she is staring at me as confused as I am about the interaction. "First off, I'm mad you didn't tell me before now. Secondly, and more importantly, WHAT THE FUCK?" She yells and I instantly start laughing.

"Right! That's what I said all night, that's also why I didn't say anything sooner, it's confusing! Hell I still don't know what to think." I tell her honestly.

We spend the next hour chatting and laughing more till we both pass out on the couch. I'm pretty sure she cuddled on top of me before she fell asleep, but I wasn't going to complain about it.

10

James

It was 2 am, when my phone chimed with a notification. As I pick it up, I see it's a sensor that shows movement in Molly's house. Opening the app, I smirk at seeing her and her friend stumble through the door. It's cute seeing her so clumsy when drunk.

Why does her friend have a familiar face? Giving myself a half shrug, *she's a realtor in the area, I must have just seen her around and not noticed till she became friends with Molly,* I tell myself.

Falling onto each other, I can tell they aren't hurt by the way she is laughing. My blood boils before I process what is happening, Molly kissed her friend, or her friend kissed her! I feel my cock twitch, yes it's most men's fantasy to be with two women but I'm not there and Molly is mine. I've never been one to share, I don't know how I feel about this.

Molly pulls away and I hear them speak softly as they decide to talk about the kiss when they are sober. *Good girl, now isn't the time to make dumb choices,* I tell my screen.

Sitting my phone down I go to the bathroom, wash my hands and head to the kitchen to get some water. When I come back the cameras have moved to Molly's room as they are changing and I pick it back up to see a little better. I don't need to invade her friend's privacy as well as hers but I'm also not paying attention to her friend. I lay down on my bed, waiting for them to finish but before I know it, sleep is pulling me under.

I wake the next morning to my alarm. It's 5 am and my phone is beside me on the bed, I glance at it and the girls are curled up on Molly's couch sleeping sound. It's Sunday so I assume they will sleep as much of the hangover away as possible. Turning my alarm off, so I can go back to sleep. Sunday is the one day I give myself to be lazy and stay in bed all I want.

Monday morning rolls around and my crew is ready and waiting at the Quartan house, Molly's house, at 6:45 am. They know I like to start at exactly 7 am and after five years of doing this, I have some really strong teams that don't need me to direct them at every move. Most of them have been with me for a few years now so that helps a lot.

I take the next 15 minutes to give them a briefing of the demolition we'll be doing over the next few weeks or so. Explaining that we are taking it slow since we don't know the condition of the studs and floor joist, the last thing I want is for someone to get hurt. Everyone is assigned an area with a lead of that area in case they have issues, everything can be reported to repairs that the lead will track for me through the day. As the smaller teams move to look at what they are working with, I go to the back of my truck and pull out two signs. One will go at the entrance of the driveway and the other will go here, where we all park, at the clearing in case someone missed the first one. They are simple, just stating unless previously authorized and qualified, the property is off limits during demolition. I always let the local law enforcement know, I have had a couple situations where I needed them, no one was arrested but they were escorted off the property. Part of my contract that all my clients sign, agree to staying off the property during this time, for their safety.

Molly on the other hand, well I adjusted the contract after checking her credentials, she can come and go but only during business hours. No one needs to be here late of an evening, not even her. She agreed reluctantly, without sass which surprised me. Like summoning the devil, she drives up as I am putting the first sign in the middle of the driveway. She turns and drives slowly around me to park beside my truck.

She smiles at me as she exits her car, "Good morning James. I won't be here long. I just need to draw up a few things in the green house and put some tarps up so I can see what I am working with." She is so cheerful this morning and it almost makes me smile, until I remember that it's probably because of her night out with her friend.

"Perfectly fine, my men are already inside." I turn to finish what I'm doing and grab the other sign.

"Please make sure they know what walls I do and don't want taken out. I don't feel like spending more money on simple mistakes." She sighs and rolls her eyes at me.

"I promise, we have gone over every detail, big and small and they are taking it slow so we can check everything before just ripping it out and spending money we don't need. They are good at what they do and follow directions better than most. To top it off I know what I am doing." I snap back. She isn't going to walk all over my team because she is a brat with me.

"You're right, I'm sorry. This is just my dream home and I'm nervous. You know what I want and I trust you." I don't miss the way she looks at me almost shyly through her lashes.

Letting out a sigh myself, "It's fine, and I do know what I am doing and I know exactly what you want. I will take care of you." I have a smirk on my face. I know she is reading between the lines because I can see the blush creep onto her cheeks. Leaving those little innuendos are fun, but most women don't pick up on them so fast.

"Okay, yea. Uumm, I'm going to get out of your way then." She turns on her heels and I can't help but watch her mosey off to the back corner of the house where the greenhouse is. I swear she has a little more sway in her hips as she turns the corner of the house out of sight. I see her glance over her shoulder one more time, and the coy smile on her face makes me want to follow her.

Instead, I do the smart thing and keep away from her and head to the end of the drive to place my other sign before heading into the house to see how the guys are feeling about the studs and joist. My eyes keep wandering to the windows and back door thinking about what Molly is doing in that greenhouse.

I can go sneak a look and see if I can catch a glimpse of her ideas. Maybe she can use some of the stuff we are tearing out that is still in decent condition. I ask the guys to save anything they think might be able to be reused for small projects and put it in a pile to the side before I slip out the back door to go to the greenhouse.

11

Molly

Out in the greenhouse, I have taken the pictures and hung the tarps to try and keep it private while I am out here working. It's hot in here so I will probably be in my sports bra and shorts as the weather warms up. I don't need James' crew to see more than they are supposed to. I won't admit that I wouldn't mind if James saw more again though. I still have a lot of questions about him, but I can still admit he is attractive and I'd love to ride that, even just once.

Ever since he was in my room after my shower. I can't shake the feeling of his hands on my body, the sensation his fingers left on my skin was like fire burning my skin. I would be lying if I said I haven't touched myself thinking about him, a lot more than even I want to admit. I feel like he is everywhere in my room and damn it turns me on, like he is watching me as I touch myself or listening as I moan his name when I orgasm. I don't know why but sometimes I freak myself out thinking he is outside my house watching me, I swear I see a shadow move outside my window. Not that I mind too much though, I always finish either way before I check which is dumb and I know it.

I sit down and grab my sketch pad, using my measurements to draw out what I am going to do in here. I have a friend from the military that makes stained glass windows now and he is going to make me a wall that faces the west and a couple small windows in the front. I decided I am going to turn this into more of a sunroom and not a greenhouse. I don't garden a lot so I think a nice sunroom will work a lot better for me. It isn't far out the back door which is off the kitchen so I can make my morning coffee and come out to relax before my day starts. Maybe when James' crew starts to landscape I can have them do a path out to here.

Drawing a little more about what I want, my mind absentmindedly goes to James again. Since I'm alone I let it wander and shut my eyes inhaling deeply. The idea of being caught is such a turn on.

I imagine James behind me, running one hand through my hair, moving it to the side to lick the bead of sweat on my neck as his other hand snakes around me and roughly rubbing my pussy through my pants. Rocking into his hand I beg 'James please,' moaning for him.

I move my hand into my shorts and lean back farther onto the table I am setting on. Resting my upper back and head against the wall. Thinking about his hand in my hair, fisting it and holding me still while his other hand slips into the waistband of my shorts, and running his finger through the slick wet folds. Dropping my head into his hold, I pant for him. 'Oh so fucking wet for me and I haven't even done anything yet.' I can hear his sultry voice in my ear as he shoves two fingers in me without warning.

Screaming from the intrusion and I buck my hips against him feeling his cock against the back of my head and...

Something hit the side of the greenhouse and I jump up gasping. "Hello?" I say loudly. I see a shadow run towards the woods before I can think to move.

I gather my stuff and stare at the door, what if they are still out there? What if I have a stalker?

Don't be stupid, you know you don't, I laugh to myself before shaking my head and slowly heading out the door. My hands are still shaking as I step out into the morning sun, I see one of James' crew standing on the back porch.

"Excuse me, did you see anyone near the greenhouse while I was in there?"

"No ma'am, sorry I stepped out for some fresh air. Is everything ok?" He cocks his head and looks around like he is looking for something.

"Yea, just paranoid lately I guess." I give a weak chuckle.

The man just smiled wide at me, "That can happen after a big purchase like this," He gestured towards the house, "But it will calm down after you see things start to come together."

"Thanks, I'm out of here for the day. You all be safe." I go to walk away but stop and turn back to him, "What time do you all show up? I was thinking I would bring coffee and donuts for everyone in the morning."

"Ma'am that's not necessary.." He takes a moment to give a dramatic pause before he smiles, " but if you really want to, we're all here by 6:35 for a briefing at 6:45."

"Thank you, I will keep that in mind, have a good day." I smile and wave as I turn to walk back towards my car, keeping an eye on the woods for movement.

Maybe I am just paranoid.

12

James

I made it back to my truck in time to see Molly talk to someone who was out back. Sounds like Derek, happy he didn't see me, the man wouldn't lie for me if his life depended on it but that's what I like about him.

I'm going through some random papers I found in my truck as I see Molly round the house, she is watching the woods. She must have seen my shadow run into them. The corner of my mouth pulls up to smirk involuntarily but I shake it off before she can see.

"Leaving so soon?"

"Umm, yea I think I've got what I need for today." I can hear the nervousness in her tone.

"That's good. Since you won't tell me what you're doing with the space, I asked the guys to save stuff they think could be good enough to be reused. If you don't want it or need it, we'll just toss it."

I see the playful smile playing at her mouth and her eyes light up, "Oh, that was nice, I appreciate it, thank you. I could probably use some of it, I am going to be putting an insulated floor in so I think anything straight will help and obviously it will be more cost effective."

At least I'm not the only one who feels this inconsistency of feelings between us. I can see it all over her. She doesn't know what to think of me and I don't know what to think of her either. It's honestly infuriating.

"Oh I'm sure there are plenty of straight ones, should be plenty long enough too." I give a wolfish grin and I see the blaze in her eyes as she catches what I was hinting at. I feel my cock twitch in my pants, why the hell do I do this to myself. I should keep my distance with her looking into me but I want to consume her, destroy her for anyone else. I feel this need to claim her.

She is blushing and trying to hide her smile, "Ok I am getting out of your hair but I am going to bring coffee and donuts tomorrow for you and the crew. Just a thank you, so I'll probably be here before ya'll." She says over her shoulder as she goes to get in her car.

I tip my head to the side as she looks to the woods one more time before turning around to leave and I feel my cock jerk. I wait till she is out of sight and make sure my truck door is blocking my view.

Unzipping my pants and pulling my cock out all I can think about are the quiet moans and the way she said my name while she was fingering herself in the greenhouse. The gap in the traps was just big enough, I could see exactly what she was doing. I wish I could have seen what she was imagining. Does she imagine me taking her rough like I want to? If I hadn't have accidently kicked the side of the building when I shifted to stroke myself, I had a perfect view of her hand in her pants, legs wide open on that table and her head tipped back, I could have watched her orgasm with my name on her lips.

Gripping my cock firmly, I stroke a few times and that's all it takes to come in my hand. The image of her is going to be burned into my head. It's not helping me stay away, but neither is watching her through her bedroom window.

I feel a shutter to my bones before I reach into the truck to grab the paper towels that are always under my center console and clean the cum off my hand and dick. I still feel wired from the sight of her, like just watching her isn't enough. I want to feel how tight she is around me, taste her for more than a second and take that little ass I know no one has fucked before. I want her to feel me for days. I am going to lose my mind if I don't fuck her. Maybe I should just fuck her and get her out of my system, but would that stop her from looking into things she needs to stay away from?

After I clean up I head back into the house to see how the guys are feeling about the house and demo. I let the team leads know I'm taking off for the day, it's only 11:30 but they know I usually jump site to site to check on things. Once I know it is all good I head to my truck, texting all the leads on the other jobs to check if they need anything. Everyone seems to be good so I head out of Molly's drive to go home. I have some calls to make and no one needs to hear this.

Once home, I ensure doors are locked and go to my home office. I opened a false door in the back of my desk. I built this desk for this purpose only, no one knows about this hiding spot and even if someone flipped it, they wouldn't find it. Taking a deep breath I pull out the lock box and unlock it with a unique key that I had made before I left my old life. I had planned for anything and everything, without telling anyone what I was doing.

In the box is a 45 caliber gun, a bunch of paperwork detailing my old life, my real identification, and an untraceable disposable phone that I have to activate for this call. I have probably 15 of these phones but I don't want to use them unless I have to and this thing with Molly, well I classify this as an emergency.

Activating the phone, I dial the only number I need, I've had it memorized my entire life. The phone only rings once, no one calls this number, no one knows this number except my father, my brother, Bash and myself. This is the only person I can trust to keep his mouth shut.

Taking a deep breath, "I need some help." Is all I say and he doesn't hesitate.

"Boy, you know your father will kill us both if he knows I talked to you. For fuck sake, he has a kill order on your head! What's the fucking issue?" I can almost feel the anger through the phone and it gives me chills. He isn't a good man but he's a better man than my father.

"You know I wouldn't have called if I didn't think it was necessary. There is someone looking into me, she knows I 'appeared' 5 yrs ago but she is snooping and I don't want her asking questions that may or may not lead back to the family. Can you change that for me?" I snap at him, not smart but the family bring out the side that I work hard to hide.

Letting out his breath like he was holding it, "Yea, it might take me a couple hours but I will make it happen and I'll send you the information so you can keep your story straight. Don't call again and get rid of the phone." The line goes dead. I know he will take care of me, he is the only one that has ever been on my side other than Bash.

After getting dressed, I put on very little makeup, just enough to make my eyes pop. I have brown eyes but they have pretty gold spots so I never really overdo my makeup and just enhance the gold.

I grab my bag and shoes from my room, double checking that I have my wallet, laptop and phone. It's only 5 am but by the time I make it to the pastry shop in Liberty and back to my house it will be nearly 6:30, perfect time to set everything up for the crew to get there.

As I slide in my car, I can smell James' cologne. It's like he was in my car, but I know he wasn't, he doesn't even know where my parents house is. I shake my head imagining it, starting the car I take off over to Liberty to go by a bakery I had ordered pastries and copious amounts of coffee from. The owner was extremely, she just opened a shop and was struggling to get her name out there. I like supporting small local businesses so I had to order from her.

Entering the parking lot, I see Jaz sitting at a table, looking at her phone in the bakery. I park my car out front of the bakery and as I enter, I smile at Jaz. "Good morning sunshine," I say, giving her a hug. "How are you today?"

Jaz smiles wide, "Well good morning gorgeous!" She gives me a quick peck on the cheek.

"I decided I would get pastries and coffee for James and his crew today."

Jaz laughs, "Well, you're definitely braver than most. I have heard from other clients that he will completely cut the woman off at a jobsite. It's like he thinks he is too good for them to speak to him."

I stare at her almost in disbelief, "Well since it is just me that bought the house, he has no choice but to deal with me. I have no problem pushing his buttons if he wants to be a jerk to me for no reason."

Just as I finish my sentence, a woman comes from the back. I turn to her and smile, "Hello, I am Molly Dowes. I ordered 8 gallons of coffee and 4 dozen mixed pastries." She laughs out loud before answering me. "Oh yes, is your car close? I can help you load it all."

Jaz, stands up, "Let me help also, I was finished anyways." She smiled and walked to the counter to help me.

"Hey, if you aren't too busy, would you like to help me set it all up at the house and see what I am planning for the greenhouse?"

Jaz looked at me almost amazed, "DUH. Plus, I want to see this James jerk for myself. I want to eye fuck him too" I laugh as she elbows me in the ribs lightly.

"Well don't eye fuck him too much." I can't help but roll my eyes as she fans herself in disbelief.

"I would never! You wound me, but I may a little." She nudges me in the side with a wild grin on her face.

We start giggling like little girls as we load everything into my car. She sends a text to her office letting them know she won't be in today as she slides into my car. We pull out of the parking lot, laughing and joking.

"But really, have you found out anymore about him?"

"Yeah, I guess I didn't put in the right information the first few times. I found out his parents died in a car accident in California when he was 20 and he went to trade school for construction. I think I was making myself paranoid for no reason." I tell her but it all still feels weird for some reason.

"Well that's good and I told you it was nothing."

We finish the drive in light talk, she keeps smiling at me and I can see the questions about this past weekend in her eyes.

"Just so you know, I do like you, like I like you like you. I hope that isn't weird." She states in almost a whisper.

Reaching over I grab her hand and intertwine my fingers with hers. "Just so you know, I like you like you too. It's all new to me, so can we take it slow?"

"Of course, on two conditions." She doesn't even wait for me to answer before she continues. "One, we will go as slow or fast as YOU want and we both can sleep with other people. I like you and I want you but I also like dick and I want that too, at least till we figure out what this is." She gestures between us, " And two, if we don't work out we stay friends. I don't want to lose our friendship."

Giggling, I glance at her, "Definitely fair. I don't want to give up dick either and we will always stay friends."

I can feel her beaming beside me as she leans over and kisses my neck, a small moan escaping my lips, "Good, then we've agreed."

It's 6:30 in the morning by the time we make it to the house, the sun is barely trying to crest behind us as we drive through the trees to the house. Reaching the house, James is already there and looking at something in the back of his truck, Jaz and I just stare at each other for a moment as I slow my car down.

"Damn girl, you didn't mention he was this sexy," she is grinning from ear to ear as she glances at me. "I hope you do fuck him, if not can I? Oh better yet, all of us!"

"Now that would be a good night for the books, that's for sure!" I blurt out laughing.

James turns as we come closer, raising one eyebrow. As we stop, he slowly approaches the driver side of the car. After I put the car in park, before I can think about it, he opens my door with a mischievous smile. I can feel the blood rushing to my cheeks, "Good morning James, I figured I the crew would appreciate pastries and coffee," I say trying to smile without showing my embarrassment from blushing.

"Oh, I can see that and it smells delicious" I can hear his playful tone and it's almost seductive.

James grins like he has a plan brewing and I'm part of it, "Let me grab that table for you and I'll set it up. The men should be starting to trickle in at any moment. They will be happy to see this so stick around for thank you's, they'll want to show proper appreciation." He says licking his bottom lip and fuck me that is the sexiest thing I have ever seen.

He has this devious smile, and for some reason it excites me. He takes the table out of my car and sets it up between my car and his truck, as he turns around Jaz is a few steps behind him, eyeing him from head to toe. "Oh, hi. I'm so sorry I didn't see you get here." James said, almost irritated as he eyes her suspiciously.

Jaz just smiles and obviously senses tension, "Hi, I'm Jaz. I sold Molly the house." She left it at that as she moved around him and set some pastries on the table and turned back to the car. I'm getting more pastries out as she rounds the car, "Girl, he is mesmerized by you, I say go for it. He is fine! And maybe some.... Personal attention would help ease the tension." She whispers and I just laugh and walk past her shaking my head, but I can see him staring at me. I gasp and stop in my tracks.

Before I can think of walking again, James is grabbing the pastries out of my hand, his hand lightly brushing down my arm and the feeling of electricity jolts through me like a tidal wave. He did that on purpose, but I can't tell the intentions. He has this burning in his eyes but his smile is wolfish, like he is going to devour me. I just shrug it off and as we finish setting up, the crew is showing up.

Good they are here to distract me.

I finish what I came to do sitting out coffee and pastries, thank everyone for being here, telling them I know this is going to be a long process and I am happy to help however I can but I will stay out of the way so they can start their day. As Jaz and I walk around the corner of the house I feel his eyes on me so I link my arm through Jaz's and lean into her a little more than needed. After we are out of view I sigh and she laughs so hard I feel it vibrate through her.

"You just had to give him a show, didn't you? I could feel him watching so I knew what you were up to." She is laughing and shaking her head at me.

I shrug off her comment as I laugh and lead her to the greenhouse. I tell her about my plans and what all is going to change as we get to the door. Unlocking and opening it for her, nothing is in here but it makes me feel better that it gets locked.

"That sounds beautiful, if you need a housemate to share this big ole place with I am more than happy to disappear into this oasis with you." She smiles and as soon as the door shuts behind us, I hear her gasp.

"Wow, I can see what you meant. This is beautiful and if you insulate it, it really is going to be the best place to sit and relax." She beams as she spins looking at the area. I assume she is trying to envision what all I wanted to do with the place.

It really is big and open. I can see this being my favorite spot on the property. As she turns to face me again, a smile on both our faces, she leans in and kisses me. Soft and deep. We slowly stumble against the table that is against the wall, the same one I was on yesterday.

Her hands are around my waist and mine are around her neck as we just stand there and make out for a few minutes. Once she slightly pulls back, I do too, both of us grinning from ear to ear.

"We agreed slow, but I've wanted to do that since I saw you walk into the pastry shop this morning." She pecks another kiss on my nose and it makes me giggle.

"Well what if I want to move a little faster? Something about this place makes me hot and bothered." Biting my bottom lip, I gently rub her arm.

"Oh?" She leans in and barely kisses my neck on the soft spot just below my ear and it makes me shiver. "And what would you like to do?"

She whispers as she continues kissing my neck and I can feel her hand rubbing against my thigh.

Moaning softly, "I want you." is all I manage to get out. Feeling her smile against my neck, I gently rock my hips towards her.

"Mmm, well how about since I've been with women before, you let me have you this time?" Her hand moves between my legs and I rock against her. "If you're not ready, we will stop, but I would be more than happy to sit you on this table and eat you till you're shuttering against me." She nips at my ear and I moan leaning into her more.

"Yes. Please. Now." My breaths are shallow and I feel an overwhelming desire to have her as close as possible .

She slowly starts kissing down my neck while her hands trail up my shirt. Lifting my arms, she slides my shirt off painfully slow as she kisses and licks the top of my breast. I want to feel the velvet tongue everywhere. Before I realize what is happening I feel my bra loosen and Jaz's mouth is latched over my nipple. Gasping and pushing into her more I let out a moan much louder than I expect and I feel her smile against me.

Letting my nipple go, she stands to kiss me again and I can't help but reach under her shirt to feel her skin.

Smiling against my mouth, "No no, this is about me taking care of you. From this point on, if you want me to stop, just say it and I will." All I can do is nod. I want her more at this moment than I think I have ever wanted anyone before. I feel her hand sliding down my body, slowly unbuttoning my pants. I reach behind me to lean against the table a little as she pushes my pants down my legs, kissing them as she crouches in front of me.

"Get up on the table." she commands as she crouches slightly, lifting me to help me onto the table and fuck me it's sexy for her to take control. Doing as she says, she slips my sandals off and then my pants and underwear, folding them slightly to sit beside me.

I gasp when she starts kissing back up my legs, but this time she is on the inner part of my legs and I spread them apart to make room for her. Moaning as she makes it to my mid thigh on my right leg, her hand starts to slowly move closer to my slit and I can feel the wetness drip through my folds. Moving myself closer to the edge, her middle finger slips in me and I moan, rocking my hips against her hand, I feel her hum as her tongue flicks against my clit.

Sliding her finger out, her tongue runs from my folds to my clit and I let out a broken sigh. I'm going to orgasm from just the buildup alone if she keeps touching me like this.

"Mmm fuck, you're so much sweeter than I thought you'd be." she says right as she sucks my clit into her mouth. Rocking against her face, I can feel her smile as she pushes two fingers in me.

"Fuckk, I'm going to come alre..." I moan breathlessly as I feel my orgasm come to a peak, my control slipping. Jaz begins to pump her finger in and out a little faster and I lose it. My legs start to shake as she sucks harder and I can feel the orgasm start to drip out of me. Moaning and shaking, she lets go of my clit and licks through my folds again, dipping her tongue in me and I grind against her. Reaching down I take a hold of her hair to ride her tongue through the last of my orgasm.

"Good girl."she hums as she praises, still licking my pussy as I shutter against her. Standing, she leans in to kiss me and I taste myself on her tongue.

"You should probably get dressed. We don't need someone to catch you like this." She tells me before kissing me again. I smile and bend over to get my clothes to get dressed, making sure everything looks how it's supposed to before we leave.

"I'm all of a sudden famished. Want to go get brunch?" I ask since I know she is free today.

"Well I probably should since I had dessert." She winks at me and we both start laughing. "But really, how about Chili's?"

"Oh yes, that sounds good." I link my arm in hers and we head to leave.

As we step out of the greenhouse, I turn and lock the door again, as I turn back around she kisses me again before taking my hand. "Thank you for sharing this with me."

I smile, "Duh! You're my best friend." As we turn, standing less than 30 feet away is James, with a devilish smirk on his face like he knows what we just did. I can feel the blush rush across my face.

"Well then, looks like you ladies had a good start to your day." Is all he says but I see him adjust himself before he turns around.

"Oh we have, maybe next time you can join us since you seem to enjoy the show so much." Jaz blurts out as I stand there shocked and bug eyed.

James stops dead in his tracks. He turns around so fast he is a blur in my vision, he made it in front of us in five strides. Grabbing us both by the wrist he pulls us to the side of the greenhouse where no one can see.

"James.." is all I get out before he lets go of our wrists, grabbing us both by a fist of hair in each hand and pulls us against the side of the building, pinning us with his body. He kissed me with such force and unfiltered passion, I felt the fire within him burning me as his tongue forced its way into my mouth.

"I'm done playing, little lamb." Is all he said before he turned his attention to a gapping Jaz and did the same thing to her. By the end of his kiss with her, he pulls me to them without thinking and we are all trying to kiss each other, each fighting to get more. Soft moans escape from all of us, tasting me on both of them, feeling James become more ravenous with each swipe of his tongue.

James pulls back trying to catch his breath. He stares at me, "I want to devour and ruin you for anyone else." Then he turns to Jaz, "If she wants you, then I want you just as bad. I am done playing. I get what I want!" he says to us both with such melting desire, before releasing us.

"Now leave before I fuck you both for my entire crew to hear because I swear I will murder them all if they even look at either of you too long, let alone see what belongs to me!" He growls at us in warning. I can feel the desire in myself build, looking over to Jaz, I can see the lust in her eyes also.

With that he turns and stalks to the house without looking back. He seems so angry now when just a moment ago, I could feel something more primal and lust filled radiating off him.

Jaz and I are still leaning against the greenhouse dazed and gasping for air before she looks at me and breaths, "Well fuck me, I guess a decision was just made for us."

I'm still breathing hard but I laugh, like a genuine laugh and it surprises me how much I'm ok with this. I think I am shocked but something about this feels oddly right.

The next few days fly by. Demolition is going great, they have gutted the house, and are about to start replacing the floors, studs, reinforcing the ceilings from walls being torn out and starting on electrical and plumbing.

I stop by almost daily to see how things are going, though I don't go inside since there is so much laying around. I don't want to get in anyone's way, and I've also been asked not to by multiple workers. They aren't mean about it, I can tell they don't want to see me get hurt, so I respect that. James has been there to greet me everyday, letting me know what is going on, staying on budget and everything like that. He has also made it a point to touch me every chance he gets, I have noticed. My hand, arm, or the small of my back when showing me the new layout of the house or handing me something. Any time he gets a chance he does, but only when no one is around to notice.

Today is no different, as I get out of my car, James comes gliding out of the house, almost like he was watching for me. Opening the back door of my car, I grab a few things to take around to the greenhouse. As I am standing up James takes up position behind me, I feel his hand gently run along my hip and skim my ass, feeling my skin heat and the electricity follow the trail. I spin on my heels to be greeted with a wicked smile plastered on his face.

"Sorry, I didn't mean to startle you. I was just coming to give you an update and see if you needed any help carrying anything to the greenhouse today." James says with such a gentleness in his tone, I almost forget that he has a way of going from being nice to an asshole in 2 seconds flat.

"Oh, well I appreciate the offer but I am good, thank you. I'm just going to be pulling out all the old stuff and getting ready for Jaz and I to start the rest." Explaining, before I shimmy past him. But before I can get far, James grabs my elbow. It wasn't hard, just enough to make me pause, and I swear I see desire in his eyes and it takes everything in me to not melt as I clench my legs, feeling my own desire build within me and the moisture build between my legs.

I can feel James tense and say, "Why do you seem on edge around me? Do I make you nervous? Or is it just that I arouse you too much? Give me half a chance, I bet your friend and us can have some fun. Or..." He drags the word out before continuing, "Just us." His cocky smile makes me want to smack him.

He knows he gets under my skin, and not in a bad way, but I feel like he is hiding something still but I want him nonetheless. I don't know if I trust him, there is something dark about him, it's intoxicating and consuming but unsafe and feral all at the same time. I looked into him a little, before 5 years ago James Felden didn't exist but then 2 days ago a bunch of stuff just appeared, much like him. I want to know what he is hiding but I can tell it's definitely something.

I pull my arm back to me and smile, "You're full of yourself aren't you? First off, you seem like the kind of man that likes to get around and I won't allow myself or Jaz to be another notch on your belt. Second, I just come here to do what I need and check on your progress. Why would you assume that I want you and I'm not here to do as I need to do. I told you I would be here to work on my greenhouse, not like I'm here to try and win your attention."

At least he doesn't know what I do with myself in the greenhouse or at home alone, is all I can think.

"Because, even though you come to the greenhouse, I've seen you watch me. I see how your breath catches around me and you seem to day dream staring at me. So tell me, why?" he says with a smirk as he cocks his head and I can't help but think what he could do with that mouth.

"You're definitely an arrogant asshole, aren't you? I do tend to daydream, and just because you drone on and on about meaningless duties and I get bored, doesn't mean I day dream about you, maybe it's about how well Jaz eats me." I throw him a sly smile, "Not like I throw myself at your feet and beg you to fuck me like you own me. I come here, to MY property to do what I need to do. I would think you know how to be more professional." I decided to be a smart ass because I have thought about it, him owning me, using me, him with Jaz and I. How intoxicating his touch is, how much more intoxicating his cock would be in me and Jaz straddling my face while they kiss and he fucks me.

"Is that so? I think you're lying, I think you do think about me and I think you think about me and Jaz with you. I would ask if you let Jaz touch my pussy yet, but I already know you let her eat you in the greenhouse." He steps closer and I didn't realize my breath caught. He smiles wickedly, an all knowing smile that makes me want him more, "see, you can't even breathe right when I step closer. The things I would do, make you beg me to stop while telling me no but your body is screaming yes. I will let you go do whatever you came to do though, but know I will fuck you before too long and then you can fuck Jaz and I together. I have to check on my men anyways."

I see him adjust himself, and wow. If he is half as big as I think, he would hurt but I can't help but wonder how amazing that stretching burn would feel. I start smiling without thinking, as I look up to him, he is smiling back and winks as his finger quickly brushes against the seam of my pants. Then he turns and walks back into the house and I feel the blush flood my face.

I head to the back of the house where my greenhouse is and hurry inside, shutting the door behind me. Why does he get under my skin? I can't help but feel the moisture soaking through my panties.

I look around to make sure no one can see in, checking all the possible cracks in the tarps and sitting in the chair that I have in here.

Lifting my dress and spreading my legs, I close my eyes and think of his hands, his mouth, his words and his tongue gliding over me.

I move my panties to the side, feeling the slickness between the folds of my pussy. I am already throbbing, thinking about his fingers sliding in me as I push one in. I gasp thinking about him nipping and sucking on my clit and I message my inner walls, adding another finger and moan. Rocking back and forth on my hand thinking about his mouth and before I realize it, my orgasm is ripping through me, "fuck yes, James, yes!" I am moaning so loud I have to cover my mouth with my other hand.

After I come down from my quick orgasm, I readjust my panties and dress. I no longer want to work on this project, so I decided to look into James Felden, or whatever his name is, more. I need to know what he is hiding.

Who is James Felden?

I hear a noise outside the greenhouse and I jump to my feet and look around but I don't see anything, it must be my imagination again I tell myself shaking it off.

After about 45 minutes of looking at my phone, searching for anything on James, my head starts to hurt. "fuck it," I say and decide to call Jaz. I need food and maybe drinks. It's 3 in the afternoon and I could use some us time, not thinking about him more than I already do.

Jaz answers on the first ring, "Hey girl, what are you doing?" she always sounds so happy and full of life.

I let out a long breath, "Well, it has been a day and I need a girl date. Do you have plans tonight? I was thinking dinner and drinks?"

"Oh, now that sounds like a plan. I am finishing work and I can meet you at the Red Door in Liberty in 2 hours?"

"That sounds perfect, I will run home, shower and meet you there."

Two hours later Jaz and I are sitting at the bar eating and having a few drinks. Chatting and laughing like we always do.

"Girl, he has gotten in my head and it's annoying me. I can't be around him without thinking about fucking him raw." I exclaim, rolling my eyes.

"But really, is it that bad? I mean, just look at him! And sorry, but THOSE kisses! He is tall, sexy, and who doesn't love some mystery?" Jaz nudges my elbow as she laughs and I can see her almost swoon at remembering the way he kissed us both so possessively.

"If he wasn't an ass about it maybe, but he has this way of making me want to hate him and fuck him all at once. I just feel it in my gut that there is something dangerous, and my gut is rarely wrong." I sigh back as we pay our checks, we head to the exit. We have been hanging out for 2 hours and I still need to drive home so I can't stay longer or I will drink more and I won't be able to drive home safely.

Out of the corner of my eye, I feel someone's eyes on me. I glance over my shoulder, but I only see groups of people chatting, not seeing anyone particular and not seeing James but I feel him and it's almost unsettling.

Outside we say our goodbyes giving hugs, a kiss and making my way to my car to head home. 45 minutes later I am pulling into my parents drive, making my way inside, my head is still swirling about questions of James. So I pull out my laptop and begin doing more research.

Before 5 years ago, James didn't exist. Before 2 days ago, there was nothing on his past but then a bunch of stuff just appeared, like I had been skipping it this whole time, which I know I didn't. I'm good at research. What is he hiding? Is he running from something? The suspense of not knowing ANYTHING about James, for some reason, makes him more sexy and dangerous at the same time. I can feel my pulse start to rise and the wetness start to build more and more in my panties and I hate how my body reacts to both sides of that with him.

Why do I still feel like someone or something is watching me? And why does it turn me on? I roll my eyes at myself.

I think I had too much to drink.

The questions kept coming. But I need to get some rest or I am just going to drive myself more crazy. Setting my computer down, I decide to get ready for bed.

I saw her at the restaurant with Jaz, I may have followed her here but that is beside the point. I snuck in behind a group of guys and hid in a corner where I could see them but they would have to look really close to see me. My sweet lamb and tempting kitten just eating, drinking and giggling like I wasn't there. After I kissed them both, I knew there was no turning back. They were mine and I won't let them go. I wasn't initially attracted to Jaz but seeing Molly want her makes me want her too, though there is something oddly familiar about her.

I followed Molly home, mainly because she had too much to drink and I didn't want to not be there if she had an accident. Luckily she drove slow and didn't swerve but I'll beat her ass for drinking that much then driving home. It's unsafe and I can't lose my lamb now, not when I just got her where I need her. Jaz got a ride home from one of her co-workers that happened to be leaving at the same time. She hadn't been drinking so I knew Jaz was safe, and I checked the camera's I snuck into her house yesterday while she was at work.

How the hell did I go from obsessed with one woman to now overly possessive of two. They both have my dick in a chokehold. Ever since I kissed them both, I can't get off. Doesn't matter how much I stroke my cock or how rough I make it, it's like the asshole refuses to cum without at least Molly or even the taste of her again. I have to change this. I can't have this much built-up tension. I'll snap at the wrong person or at the wrong time. I need to take this control back.

Molly makes it home, I park a little way out of sight and sneak through the woods to her house, looking inside I see her propped up in bed on her laptop. I pull my phone out to see what she is looking at on one of the cameras. It takes me a second to find the right angle but I do and my blood boils.

Why is she still looking into me? I had information about James Feldon's past put up, she should be satisfied. I know it all seems legit because of who did it. He would never leave any holes for someone to ask more questions that can't be answered.

At that moment, my phone vibrated with a blocked email. That can only be one person and I can't check that here. I need my secure laptop which is at home.

I pocket my phone and watch her a little longer. She puts the laptop away and lays down for bed.

It's time for me to see why I am getting another email that I shouldn't be getting, to an account that no one knows about. The last thing I want to do is leave her but this could be something a hell of a lot more dangerous. Making my way to my truck, I check the cameras again to make sure both her and Jaz are sleeping, knowing they are makes me calm down a little before I head to the house.

Once home, I dig my secure laptop out of a hidden compartment in the floor. I have these spaces all over my house, all with different things like electronics, money, guns and various other things. Starting my laptop and opening my email, I see it. One email, blocked sender. I make sure all my security is up and active before I open it. No one can track me here or everything I have worked for will be gone and possibly dead.

'Boy, the information was posted but I added a little tracking to show who is looking into you.

Molly Dowes, she's young and looking at James Feldon records, she's a client.

Your father put a $20 million bullseye on your head. Watch your back, this girl is harmless, a no one, but the family is looking for you hard.

No one can find Damion Conner!'

I closed the email. This isn't good, if I know my father, he put the Miner family on me and I really don't know if that is good or bad either though. They are the most lethal family I know, but would he really kill me? After everything I put him through, maybe. That is a past that could be good to see again, but I don't know if that feeling will be returned.

I can't think about that, I need to shower and come up with a plan to get Molly off this ridiculous task she has put herself on.

After my shower, I check the information that was planted on the internet but I know it all seems legit. The link about my 'parents' accident would take you to what looks like a real accident report. The technical school is real and documents have been altered to show my attendance and graduation date. It is all as air tight as it can be. Why is she still skeptical?

Before I realize it, I pass out.

The next morning I get around and head to the office to check progress on all the jobs before I go to Molly's house to finish cleaning with the demo crew before the next crew gets there at noon. My crews are swift and efficient. As one is finishing the next is ready to start. They make me proud to see how well we all have worked together and grown. Without them, I wouldn't be where I am and I always remind them that I may be the boss but they are the ones I turn to because without them there would be no me.

At noon, my demo crew is walking out the door of Molly's house as the next crew is outside waiting to be briefed on the next steps. I gather my demo crew and tell them thanks for their hard work, giving my company credit card to the team lead and tell him to take them to lunch on me. They all cheer and shake my hand as they tell the next group of men good luck and shake hands in passing. Luckily none of my crews really have issues with anyone on any crew and that definitely makes the job easier.

The crews differ though. The demo crew is mainly all younger men ranging from 18-30 years old. I do it like that because we all start somewhere and demo is hard on the body so the younger men handle it better. The next crew is bones and repair and they range from 50-70 years old. Bill is the oldest and I wish he would retire since I don't want to see him hurt but he says he is still young enough to work and he always passes his yearly physical so I can't complain too hard. I made this crew older because they seem to be more experienced and I don't have to babysit them. They know what to do and how to do it, but they still train new people to help keep the business growing. The finishing crew is a mix of men and women, I give women the option to be on any crew like the men but the most of them that work for me like the finishing but they help on all when needed. The finishing crew does all the drywall, tiling and painting. I have a décor crew but Molly opted out of that so they have a week paid vacation that they would usually be here working.

I brief my bones crew and I hear a car coming up the drive, I have to contain a smile. My guys don't need to know my personal dealings.

Molly doesn't get out of her car immediately and after my guys go inside to start working I turn to see her looking at something in her lap. Walking over to her door, I get a glimpse of what she is planning for the greenhouse and I have to say I am impressed with what I saw which isn't much.

Once she notices me standing near her car, I see the flush cross her face as she shuts the folder she was looking at, she opens the door and steps out.

"I guess you saw my plans for the greenhouse." she cocks an eyebrow at me and it takes everything in me to not laugh, she is so cute when she questions what she knows.

"I did a little, they are really good. I am more than happy to help." Stepping into her space, I can feel the heat radiate off her.

"I know you're busy and I don't think us being trapped in that space together would be wise." She pivots around me and moves to the back door of her car to pull out some tools.

"I think it would be amazing to trap you in a room for a while." I can feel my grin become feral and my cock grow in my pants. "I already told you, I am done playing this dance around game. I get what I want and I want you!"

"Yes I heard you the first time." Her breathing is erratic and heavy. I can feel her fighting this but she wants it too and I know it.

"I'm coming for what belongs to me," I step closer to her, caging her before I push my bulge against her and she moans. I can practically feel her melt into me. "That's right baby girl, you want me as much as I want you. I'll be coming to claim what's mine and soon." I step back as I cock an eyebrow at her and wink before heading inside to work.

F uck me, James is definitely arrogant. I roll my shoulders as I grab what I need and head to the greenhouse. Once I get inside, I start taking the tarps down and clearing out the space. After I get everything outside, I see a few of the crew members walking towards me. I don't know these guys but they have a genuine smile and if they are like the demo crew, they have to be nice. They are older men. One looks to be nearly 70 and the other probably not far behind his friend. But something about the older ones' faces seems familiar.

"Molly?" the old man ask

Giving them a kind smile, "Yes, may I help you?"

"Well, you sure have grown up. You probably don't remember me but your dad and I used to build greenhouses around town together. I remember you coming to help when you were little. I'm William Bidel, but everyone calls me Bill."

"Oh my goodness! Yes I remember you, I haven't seen you since I was probably 8. I thought you and your wife, Mary if I remember right, moved to Texas." I'm beaming at my dads old friend as I give him a hug.

"Oh we did but Mary's sister got sick so we came home to help her and realized we missed it so we moved back a few years ago. Last I talked to your parents, you joined the service. Happy to see you home, I know your mom and dad missed you. What are you doing out here anyways? This little building has some good bones, I hope you aren't going to tear it down."

"No! I actually want to turn it into a sunroom," reaching for my sketch pad I show them what I am going to do. "I have an old friend from the service that is making me a stained glass wall for the west wall, and windows for the east side. I am going to make solid walls on the North and South and then I am going to do either a Plexiglass or tempered glass roof." I can feel the excitement coming off me in waves, but Bill and dad did some amazing things so if anyone can give me insite when dad isn't here, it will be this man.

"Well I'll be, that's going to be something special. Sorry I didn't want to interrupt the reunion, I'm Kyle, Bill's brother." He reaches his hand out to shake mine.

Taking his hand and smiling at him, now that I look I can see the similarities. "It's so nice to meet you and thank you. I have put a lot of thought into this building. The demo crew left me a lot of good pieces of wood that I am going to use to frame and build an insulated floor and redo a few studs in the walls before I insulate them a little. I just have to get the time off work to get it done." I chuckle and roll my eyes.

Bill and Kyle exchange a look but they both smile at me.

Over their shoulders, I see James and he looks pissed.

"Well I don't want to keep you all any longer plus James looks mad that you're out here and not in there.. I'm happy you said hi, it was great seeing you." I laugh because I have a feeling that's not true at all but I don't want to tell them that.

"Yea, we need to get back in there. It was wonderful seeing you too, tell your folks hi for me." Bill smiles as they both turn to go back to the house.

I spend the rest of the day cleaning around the green house and going through the scrap lumber to find good pieces to reuse. Setting the better ones in a smaller pile off to the side and covering all with a trap to keep it dry through the night.

Looking at the time on my phone it's nearly 5 in the evening and I am getting hungry. Just as I am about to call Jaz, James walks out of the house towards me.

"Molly, call Jaz. I'm taking you both to dinner." He is smirking at me but before I can object he continues. "There is a little bistro at the river market, I will text you the local. Meet me there at 7. Both of you."

And he just turns towards the front of the house without another word and strolls away like he doesn't have a care in the world.

I stand there stunned, phone in my hand when it rings. Looking down I see it's Jaz.

"Hey, I was about to call you."

"Well since I got a weird message from James, I figured I would see what is going on." Jaz says and I can hear her skepticism.

"That asshole! I was about to see if you wanted to go to dinner and he marched over to me, TOLD me he was taking you and I to dinner and to be at a bistro at the river market at 7. Then he just walked away. What the hell is wrong with him."

Jaz just laughs, "Babe, its food, with a man that wants us both. Maybe we should hear him out and it's not like we both don't want him. We have both agreed that we would. Plus who doesn't love a free meal?"

Rolling my eyes and sigh heavily, "Fine. Do you want me to pick you up?" I can hear myself pouting but I don't care.

"No, I have a showing, it should be done at 6:30 so I'll meet you all there, just send me the location..." she trails off, "Never mind, James just sent it to me."

I didn't give the girls an option if they wanted to come to dinner with me. We need to discuss this situation between the three of us like adults. It doesn't help that I can't get them off my mind so I need to clear the air.

It is 6:45 as I park near the bistro and go inside. I made a reservation so we have a private room. I make my way inside, telling the hostess my name and I am escorted to the room. I pick a seat facing the door and wait for both women to join me.

Within 5 minutes, the door opens again and both women walk in and my breath is taken away. They are stunning and MINE, whether they are fully aware of it yet or not. I can feel the feral grin on my face grow along with the bulge in my pants and I have to readjust myself before I stand. I walk around the table to pull out their seats, "Ladies, happy you found the place."

They both say thank you as they set and I make my way back to my seat letting my fingers skim over both their shoulders. Fuck me they smell like sin and I need them both. I have to remind myself that we are here to talk first. I have to get them on board with this idea I have.

After I sit down, I can't help but let my eyes wander over them both. Molly shifts under my gaze and I see Jaz reach over and set her hand on Molly's thigh. My gaze burns trying to see through the table to see where I want my hands on them both.

They are wearing dresses, Molly went home to shower and change after sweating in the greenhouse all afternoon but I assume Jaz came from work. Molly is in a simple navy blue form fitting dress, it's flattering but not overly revealing and it looks devine on her. Jaz is in a perfect black pencil skirt with a light gray blouse, it all hugs her beautiful curves like it was painted on her.

The waitress comes into the room, "Good evening, I'm Maggie and I'll be your waitress. Can I start you off with drinks and an appetizer?"

Molly and Jaz both ask for red wine and I get a scotch on the rocks.

The waitress leaves to get our drinks, coming back a moment later with them and we order our food. Once the waitress leaves, I sit in my chair.

"Now that we have a moment, I'm going to be honest. You both have figured out that I want Molly, and if you," Looking directly at Molly, " want Jaz I'm fine with that. I want you first though. Then I want both of you. You can be together without me all you want but I want you both." I tell them pointedly.

They both suck in a deep breath but Molly is the first to speak.

"And what makes you think, I want you without Jaz." She gives me a smirk that tells me she is trying to push my buttons.

"Oh I'm good with you fucking us." Jaz quirks an eyebrow with a teasing grin on her face and I can't help but growl.

"Jaz!" Molly shrieks at her and it almost hurts my ears at how high pitched it was.

"What? You wanted him before we knew about the others feelings. You two do you and I can be the happy bonus." The grin on her face tells me she has thought about this. Setting back I palm my cock, trying to readjust myself.

Molly watches and I can see the desire written all over her face. Then she looks at Jaz again, "I don't know. I guess I can agree if you want to. We agreed on us before we thought HE was in the mix." She gives Jaz a questioning look. I can see she is fighting herself, she wants this but she doesn't want to admit it.

She makes a pointed glare at me and I smirk.

"Good then it's agreed." As I finish my statement as the waitress opens the door with our food. We all sit back and eat with light chat about work, the waitress comes back to check on us. Finishing our meal in small talk and the girl laughing. I mainly watch them and try to ignore my cock wanting to be buried in either of their mouths.

The next time the waitress comes in I ask for the check and pay. Leaving the restaurant we all stop. Jaz turns to face Molly, "I promise I am good with all of this." She gives her a deep kiss and Molly moans into her. I feel my breath pick up but Jaz turns to me. "WE are a package. You hurt her and I will kick your ass."

I smirk at her but before I can say anything she puts one hand on my neck, pulling me to kiss her as her thigh rubs against my throbbing cock before she backs off and smiles. "Night you too. Molls I'll call you tomorrow. James, I'll see you soon." She turns on her heels and prances away.

Molly turns and looks at me laughing, "She's in a dramatic mood." Rolling her eyes but I can see her blushing under the street lights. "Well it has been a long day so I'm going home, have a good night." She goes to blow me a kiss but I grab her elbow and spin her back to me snaking one arm around her and the other into her hair and I kiss her brutally. Claiming her mouth, I growl "MINE" before I let her go.

She is panting and her hooded eyes tell me she is as turned on as I am.

Taking a step back she looks up at me. "You're crude and I feel like you're hiding something. I don't know if I trust you, completely yet." She is taking a step backwards before she turns and hurries to her car. I just stood there, stunned. She admitted to knowing I am keeping secrets but she's in for a surprise if she thinks I am going to let her go.

Tonight has been one hell of a night. Jaz and I agreed but I don't know if I can trust James yet. I want him and we all know it but I don't know if I'm ready to let him into my life with all these secrets. I need him to tell me the truth first.

Laying on my bed, about to fall asleep, I hear footsteps coming from the hall, they seem to be getting closer. I get up to get away from the door, maybe hide, or grab the bat that is in my closet but there is nowhere in this room to hide and the closest is close to the bedroom door on the other side of my bed, slowly stepping farther from the door as it slowly opens. When the person sees I'm not in bed, the door flies open slamming against the wall. James comes in, his eyes almost look wild.

As soon as he sees me he strides toward me, so smoothly it seems like he is floating. Before I could ask what he was doing, he grabbed me by the throat and pinned me to the wall. My nails scratch into his arm, but he doesn't seem to notice. He isn't hurting me but he startled me more than anything, the feral look in his eyes that is almost insatiable.

"You have been looking into me and my past. Why?" he says with rage flaring but I can't tell if it's anger or sexual. It feels like both.

My breath was shallow and my voice was low, "I don't know anything about you. I wanted to know who you are and if I can trust you with Jaz and I." Fear seeped from every word. I'm not sure what brought this on, it scares me but at the same time makes me want him more. I hate my body for betraying me right now.

"If you want to know me Molly, all you have to do is tell me. I will show you the man I am." An evil grin creeps across his face. "I will share my secrets with you but that means you are completely mine. Mine to fuck, to use, to trust and to devour."

Without releasing me, he put his hand between my legs, feeling the silky wetness dripping from my slit. His grin became more prominent. "Oh, that's how you want to know me? You want to feel me use that tight cunt don't you?" saying more of a statement than a question as he whispers it to me and I feel his breath trail my ear and neck.

I can feel the tears starting to fill my eyes, "No, that's not what I want at all! I'll stop looking!" Fear fills my chest, I have never seen him like this.

"Your sweet cunt is saying otherwise." he presses two of his fingers against my panties a little harder and it takes everything in me to not moan. "You were looking into me, this is me but I'll tell you the rest of me later. I'll take what I want now, and I can tell you want it too. Right now I NEED you and then we will talk after." His eyes trace my face down my neck as he watches my breast with every breath. "I don't want you, though. Needing you isn't even the right word. I live for you, I will kill for you if you need that. I am giving you all of me." His fingers moved my panties to the side and he roughly thrust two fingers in me. Gasping and trying to claw at his hand on my throat and push his other arm away at the same time. He is too strong, and the animalistic look in his eyes makes him seem more on the prowl for prey.

James is looking at me like a starving animal, I can't help but feel the arousal build in me, but it also scares me. I have never seen a man this primal and I want it. I need it!

His fingers slowly pull out of me, and I watch his eyes light up like a light shining on the most perfect diamond as he lifts his hand drenched in my wetness to his mouth. A growl starts deep in his chest as he licks his fingers one at a time and all of a sudden he kisses me, forcing his tongue in my mouth. "Taste yourself? That is my life source, your pussy is my holy grail, and I need to consume all of you. You are mine, you can not run, hide or even die without me. I will always bring you back to me!" He proclaimed as he lifted me into his arms and took me to my bed.

"James, please!" I beg as he drops me on the bed, in one swift motion, he rolls me onto my stomach and rips my lace panties off as if they weren't even there.

"I have watched you, the desire in your eyes as you look at me, sneaking off to the greenhouse and fingering yourself with my name on your lips." He licks the sweet spot on my neck.

OH MY GOD! Has he seen me sneak off?

"I like to peek in, watching you finger yourself, rubbing your breast and pinching your nipples. Watching your back arch as you hold your breath and right as you climax, MY. NAME. slips from your mouth," Growling as his fingers dip in my pussy and pull out as he teases my ass. I feel his length harden and massive against my ass, I am trying to remind my body that he is hiding things and I don't trust him yet but I keep getting more and more wet. I feel the arousal gliding down my thighs. I want him so bad, even if I can't admit it out loud, I do. I need him.

James is holding me down with one hand in the middle of my back. He pushes two fingers in me and I can't help but moan and lift my ass for him. I need more, I need him! "Please, I need you." I beg and I can since his smile.

"Oh, little lamb. You're about to get me. I've seen you moan and squirt on your fingers as you touch yourself in that greenhouse. Thinking of me. Now you're going to feel me and do it on my cock!" he says against my back. I can feel his tongue trace my spine and fuck I can't stop it anymore, I moan and try to push back towards him.

"You like to hold your breath, but tonight you're going to feel more, I want you to scream my name, you can TRY to get away, but you WILL squirt on my cock before I allow you to rest! I want you to squeeze every drop of cum out of me until neither of us can barely move, then I will fill that tight ass!" He pushes his fingers back into me and I lift my hips to meet them.

Feeling him shift on the bed, I can now feel his length between my ass and I gasp, "N-no one has ever fucked my ass." I breathe out nervously.

Growling, "Fuck baby, I will be gentle this time, but I need you. I need to fill all of you! I promise I won't hurt you, ever." he whispers the last word in my ear before he sits up on his knees.

He grabs both my hands behind my back and uses his belt to tie them together. I try to wiggle free, he knows what he is doing though, and I can't move my wrist an inch. He then grabs my hair and pulls me back to him, I feel his length just out of reach barely skimming my finger tips, as he smiles and kisses me on my neck. His free hand grabs my breast and pinches my nipple harder than I could imagine, but it is not bad, more like that perfect line between pain and pleasure. I felt my body light with electricity, as I saw him smile out of the corner of my eye. He growls and shoves my face into the bed as his hand keeps moving down my body. Rubbing the head of his cock against my clit, my breath catches, I wasn't expecting him to feel that big. A whimper slips from my throat. "Yes please, take me!" I begged, pushing my hips into him.

I hear him, softer than anything I have ever heard, "Take a deep breath, you are going to take everything I give you." At that moment, I feel his thick head push into me and he lets out a deep growl. Gasping for air, he pulls out and pushes back in, again and again, deeper and deeper. Harder with each thrust.

"Fuck you're too big, I can't!" my body is shaking with a burn I have never felt before and I feel the tears falling from my eyes like a waterfall as I scream with each thrust.

"Then I will split you in two, but you WILL take me," He purrs in my ear as he grabs a fist full of hair pulling my head back. "Fuck little lamb, you look perfect crying for me." He licks up from my shoulder to my ear. He pulls out again and without warning, I feel him slam in me as deep as he can. His hips pushing me harder up the bed, I let out a deep whine. "Yes, little lamb. The big bad wolf will devour you." He growls as he licks up my neck and nips my ear.

Fighting my body, fuck he feels too good and I will my body to relax to take him. He hurts so good! I felt a tingle in my stomach as he licked my neck before setting up. I feel him start to slow, making my body shake uncontrollably. His hand reaches around and pushes between me and the bed and begins to rub perfectly timed circles on my clit. I feel his other hand move to my ass as his finger circled my tight hole. Gasping, "No, you can't! It's too much!" I exclaim, begging him not to do what he is thinking.

He refuses to listen, he pulls his hand back and I hear a pop from his mouth like he sucked on his finger, then I feel it. He pushes his thumb into my ass slowly as he began to fuck me harder. I cry out, not sure if it hurts or if I like it more. It's tight, intrusive, and hurts, but it also feels good, full and intensely arousing. His finger in my ass shouldn't feel this good, and I feel him push a little more till I feel his knuckles against me and I moan. Feeling my body rock into him.

"That's right baby, you CAN take it, mmmmm and you like it. Your pussy is more soaked now." I can hear his control slipping in his tone. My body starts to respond, pushing against him, moans ripping through my chest.

"Good little lamb. Come for me, soak your cock, squirt for me baby!" He growls as he fucks me harder, his hand is still busy with a finger in my ass while the other pinches my clit. I suck in a deep breath, as I can feel my body ache for a release.

"I'm coming," slips from my lips, I can't even think straight. He uses his body to hold me down, growling against my back.

"Come now, little lamb! Come on your cock!" He growls and I can't hold it any longer. I feel myself tighten on his length. I let out a screaming cry as he pumps harder and harder. Feeling myself squirt harder than I ever had before, I feel it running down my legs and he keeps going. "YES LAMB, that's what you needed!" I ride the massive orgasm to the end, before collapsing.

I barely opened my eyes as he rolled me onto the floor on my knees, fisting my hair in his hand, "Open that pretty mouth, swallow for me. Show me how much you need my cum!" He says with a darkness in his eyes that seems inhuman.

I don't even see him move as he shoves his cock in my mouth, half of it doesn't even fit before he hits the back of my throat and I gagged but wanting to please him I force myself to relax my throat. He pumps a few times before I feel him hold tight and come, silk spurts of thick come into my throat forcing me to swallow.

Tears fell down my face but for some reason, I wasn't scared anymore. I was wet again. I needed him again, fuck he is making me insatiable. He pulls out of my mouth, bending over, and kisses me, grinning, "Good girl, little lamb. Your body wept for me, and I needed you to know who owns you now." He licks a little cum dripping out of the corner of my mouth and kisses me again, letting me clean him off his tongue and I moan for it. I want more.

He unties my hands and in one swift move he picks me up. Kissing my head, he carries me to the bathroom and sets me on the toilet. Turning, he turns on the water for a bath. Once he gets the temperature he wants, the water starts to fill and he gets in as he reaches for my hand to pull me with him.

"James, that tub is too small for both of us." I giggle but he just grins at me.

"I took you, now I will always take care of you, get in and let me wash you." he grabs my hand and pulls me gently to him. I step in between his legs and sit down. It's tight but he makes space for me. His touch is gentle as he uses a wash cloth to rub my body and clean me.

"Did I hurt you?" He asks as he kisses my shoulder. I can hear the concern in his voice and it makes me shiver.

"A little but not more than I liked, wanted or could handle." I admit with a sigh.

He kisses my shoulder again and I can feel him getting hard again. "If I ever get too rough with you or Jaz tell me! I never want to hurt either of you! I haven't let anyone close to this side of me in 6 years. You're going to have to remind me sometimes." His arms wrap around me and he holds me tight. I started to slip so I wiggled back to him again.

Growling, in a playful way, "Did you enjoy my finger in your tight ass? And be honest."

I let out a sigh, "Honestly" I paused for a moment before I smiled against his forearm, "I liked it a lot more than I thought I could. Yes, it hurt but it also felt good. I don't think I can handle your cock though."

He laughs, genuinely laughs and nips my ear, "No, that will take time. I will have to work on stretching your ass to be able to fuck you without truly hurting you." He kisses the side of my head as he stands behind me and I look over my shoulder. *HOLY HELL! He is huge! How did that fit in me?*

He reaches down and lifts me to stand. Leaning over he kisses me deeply, like he never has before.

"I want you again before we talk. Please." I can see the pleading look in his eyes. He is a completely different man than I have ever seen before, and it makes me trust him for some reason. I feel the want and need vibrating through him. I turn and step out and I can feel him on my heels.

"I won't touch your ass again tonight unless you ask, but please let me make love to you. Let me fill you with my come and then eat it out of your pussy as you writhe against my face." Pushing me out of the bathroom and back towards my bed, I let out a moan as he rubs my clit with two fingers like he knows my pussy better than I ever have.

"Fuck me James. Fuck me hard, please." I beg as I relax and lean against him.

Without second thought, he picks me up and walks me to the bed, laying me down as he drops to his knees. "I will but I am dying to taste you first." Without warning he buried his face between my legs and licked me from my ass to my clit.

Moaning, I run my hands in his hair while rocking my hips against his tongue. He nips at my clit then abruptly stands, stroking his cock and I lick my lips. James smiles again and leans over to lick me again but this time he doesn't put his tongue back in his mouth. He stands up with a glint in his eyes and leans over to kiss me. Without thinking I do what I know he wants and take his tongue in my mouth, tasting myself.

We both moaned at the same time and mid moan he shoved his cock in me in one quick motion. Reaching down he strokes my clit with one hand and his other wraps around my throat. He squeezes my throat as he thrust harder in me. "Fuck baby girl, that was sexy! Come for me! I'm not going to be able to last long, come for me so I can come!" He pinches my clit and on command my back arches off the bed and I swear I can feel my soul leave my body as I start to see stars as his grip tightens. Then with a growl I feel him thrust 2 more brutal times before his body starts to tremble and he releases my throat and braces his arms on either side of me. Kissing my neck and still breathing hard, he rolls to lay beside me.

I catch my breath before leaning over and kissing her again. Fuck she is better than I could have imagined. Setting up I find my underwear and slip them on.

"Um, what do you think you're doing? You promised to tell me the truth." I see the concern in her eyes.

Laughing I push her to lay back down. "I'm just going to get a warm washcloth to clean you up, then we will talk. Calm down, I promised to tell you, and I will. I will also NEVER break a promise I make to you."

"Oh, I thought you were about to leave." I can feel her body relax against the bed.

"On second thought, I think I will keep my word." Smiling like a mad man, I go get a washcloth, put it in a bowl of hot water and take it to her room. As I enter she is still laying there trying to calm her heart rate presumably but her eyes are shut like she is about to fall asleep. Kneeling between her legs she gasps looking down at me.

"What do you think you are doing now? I can't! Not again, please!" She pleads with me.

I smile and I can feel the feral look in my eyes. "Doing what I said I would." Before she can say more I am lapping at her pussy coated in my come. Rolling my eyes as I hum my approval.

"James, I can't come again, please." She begs again, but I know she is too tired for that already.

Licking her one last time, I set back and grab the wash cloth. I smile, "Little lamb, I know you can't come again. I told you I was going to eat both our orgasms out of your sweet cunt, and I will always keep my word with you."

Using the washcloth I gently clean her before taking my briefs back off and crawling into bed. I pull her up to lay beside me and hold her close.

"Let me start by saying, this is going to be a lot to understand but what I tell you has to stay between you and I. We will talk to Jaz later about it. I can't handle doing it again too fast." I sigh, the pain of telling anyone the truth is harder than I ever imagined. But I also never thought I would let someone back into my life again.

"Are you a serial killer?" I can feel her tense thinking that is a likely possibility.

I chuckle softly, "No, I'm not a serial killer but I won't lie and say I haven't killed. It's just been a long time." pulling her tighter to me, I can feel her relax.

"But you're running from someone, the police?"

"I am, well, more like hiding. My father and I had a falling out. I didn't agree with decisions he made, so I cleaned out my inheritance and left without a word. Let me start at the beginning or none of it will make since." I take a long deep breath, this will be the first time I have told anyone.

"My father is the head of the Conner Family Mafia in Boston. My family has been in power for over 80 years when my grandfather came over from Ireland and started the organization." I feel her try to turn to look at me so I set up and turn to face her. "In high school, I had two loves. Kelly Ivoncof, her uncle, was part of the Russian Bratva, and Bash Miner, his family has been hired hands of my family for years." I let their names set for a moment, it still hurts to think about them.

"Bash and I have been best friends our whole lives. As we got older, we experimented and realized we enjoyed each other more than just friends. In high school I met Kelly, and I loved her. Bash, being amazing, stayed my best friend and sometimes lover but he stepped back for Kelly and completely understood. Neither of our families would have been ok with him and I. My father never liked Kelly since her family and my family are always in one war or another but we didn't care. Neither of us wanted to be a part of that life and as we got older we planned on leaving and never looking back. 6 years ago, my dad had me followed. I had been ordered to never see her again but I believed that being an adult meant I could do what I wanted. It was 'time to take my place in the family business' as he always told me but I didn't want anything to do with it. So I text Kelly and asked her to meet me at our favorite spot, I left to meet her and was there in less than 30 minutes." Molly is just watching me, not saying anything but she is listening to every detail.

"Once I got there we came up with a plan to meet back in the morning and leave, we both had money stashed away for that moment. We went back to our houses but once I got home, my dad was waiting at the door and he was more calm than I had ever seen him." I turned to face her a little more. "He shot me with a perfect aim to my right side. He missed all vital organs and said, 'this will be the last time.' and I had a bad feeling. Once I was able to slow the bleeding, I called Kelly, but she never answered and never called me back. I still don't know what he did but I know deep down he had her killed."

Molly gasped and set her hand on my thigh. "What happened to Bash?"

I smile at his name, "Bash, as far as I know, is still working with his father, for mine. Somehow they never knew about us or we both would be dead, not just shot." I sigh and smile more at the memories of him.

"We never said goodbye, I knew I could trust him but his father was too loyal to mine. So I figured it was best he didn't know I was leaving. I took the next year and made a plan, telling no one, well except the one person I knew would die before he would say anything, but he is a story for another night. Anyways, when it was time, I left, and never turned back. My father is the worst of the worst. He is paranoid and dangerous but the army he has behind him makes him worse. He's killed almost all of the Russians in Boston, gaining more money and more power."

"So what is your real name?" she almost whispers like she is scared to ask.

"I know you asked a friend of yours at the FBI to look into James, but you can't in any way do that again! Please promise you will stop digging, then I will tell you."

"I can do that. For you I will stop." She wraps an arm around my waist and hugs me gently, kissing the scar of the bullet my father gave me.

"Tomorrow I will bring you a bunch of real documentation of me. Newspapers articles and everything for you to read, including pictures, birth certificate and whatever else you want, as long as you believe me. My real name is Damion Connor, only son to the infamous Caleb Connor." I sigh at the vulnerable honesty I just gave another person.

We sit and I let her process for a few moments before I say, "If what I have heard is true, I know who will be looking the hardest for me and I'm not sure if it's good or bad."

"Who?" I hear the concern in her voice.

"Bash, he is the best but he might also want answers. If he finds me, which he will, he knows me better than anyone else, I'm not sure if he will want to talk or kill me for leaving him."

"He was your first love?" The gentleness in her voice makes me smile.

"Yes, and even if he wants to kill me, I will always love him." I admit to the painful truth

With that we lay down and she is asleep within a minute. She is the first woman I have wanted since Kelly, well her and Jaz but I will protect them! No one will hurt them like Kelly was. I have to be better for them, do better protecting them.

Molly

I woke up and could immediately tell I was alone but I could also smell bacon and hear Jaz's giggling. "No, you can't use half & half in the eggs. Milk or heavy whipping cream."

"What's the difference? They all look the same." I hear James whine.

I can practically hear James roll his eyes from here and it makes me smile. This is odd but I like it. It feels natural though. Rolling out of bed, I find his button down shirt and slip it on, like I assumed, I am swimming in it but it smells like him and it feels like home.

Walking out of my room, Jaz see's me first.

"Morning babe. How are you feeling?" she literally beams as I enter the kitchen.

"Morning both of you." Looking at Jaz, "When did you get here?"

"Oh you know when the big bad wolf here called and said he doesn't know how to cook but you needed food after last night." She gives me a knowing grin with a wink.

I just roll my eyes, as she strides over to give me a kiss. Before I realized it I felt James' hand around my back and I feel him on the other side holding us both. I feel him nuzzle his head between my shoulder and neck.

"I would love to have you both as soon as possible but I do have to show up at the site today." He kisses my neck then turns and kisses Jaz. My heart feels so full with them both here. I never imagined being in a relationship with multiple people but this feels right.

Hold on, am I in a relationship with them? We haven't discussed anything like that!

Jaz giggles, "Well since I let you have her last night, it's my turn to have some fun. You can go to work and we'll be there later. I am coming to help with the greenhouse project while you and your men are inside doing the hard work." She winks at him and he growls while I just laugh at them both.

"Do NOT tempt me. I will come out and fuck you both while my men are inside. Try my patience." The look in his eyes tells me he is telling the truth and the look in her eyes tells me she wants to see how far she can push him.

"Okay you two." I'm laughing at them baiting the other. "I am going to shower and clean up, then we can have breakfast before you have to leave. Hold on, sorry that sounded relationshipy..." James cuts me off before I can finish my babbling.

"Baby, for you, this is definitely a relationship. As long as you and Jaz are happy to deal with me being a possessive asshole. As far I am concerned you both are mine and I'm not giving you up. Honestly I would prefer if you all were together more so I know where you both are at all times." he gives me a wink and pulls Jaz in closer to us.

That definitely answered my questions for him at least. Now I need to talk to Jaz about all this.

"Well, we were talking about when you get my house done Jaz could move in with me. Big house like that deserves lots of people to love it." I laugh and look at her. She definitely has a look in her eyes that is asking if I am being serious.

James pulls Jaz closer, kissing her cheek, "Good, I will pay out the contract on your apartment when the house is finished so you both can be in one place." He turns to look at me again, "And when you're both ready I'll move in, which better be soon because I don't plan on leaving your side much from now on."

He says all this like there isn't a choice but at least he said when we are ready. Jaz would be moving in as my best friend and possible partner, James on the other hand, well he is more and I can feel it but I can't move too fast. He is completely different and I think him opening up to me has taken a weight off his shoulders that he needed.

"Well, I guess you and I are going to be living together." Smiling at Jaz, "I was going to ask if you wanted to move in anyways. It would be nice to have someone else in the house with me anyways."

Jaz kissed my cheek, "Good because I was going to be there all the time anyways." She giggles but we both know she is telling the truth, she is my best friend but we have something more between us and I like that we can make this work with us and James.

"Ok, now that all that is settled, you shower and Jaz can finish breakfast while I make coffee. At least I know how to do that." James laughs as he kisses my other cheek and grabs Jaz by the hand.

Yep, this feels right.

"How do you not know how to cook?" Jaz elbows him in the side.

I can see James try not to tense at the question. "I grew up in a different lifestyle, we had a personal chef so I never had to know how to cook." giving the most vague answer he can but I know after last night that is a lot for him to give up. I'm happy he is opening up to us. Well, at least me for now.

"I know you had to have talked to Molls last night, can we talk sometime? If this is an all of us situation, I feel I deserve to know also." She almost sounds timid to ask him, like she is afraid he will say no.

"You do babe, and we will, I promise. Let me have a day to let my nerves relax and lamb and I will set down with you. Is that fair?" I can hear the concern in him but I know Jaz enough now to know something is better than nothing with her.

He is so gentle compared to the man I met a few weeks ago. I am about to shut the bathroom door when I hear Jaz respond.

"Of course. We are an us now not just you, we need to share the burdens and let us support each other. But If you need a little time between talking, whatever it is, it must have been a lot for you, take your time. If Molly can trust you and I trust her, then I trust you too." she leans into his shoulder and I can see that she has relaxed.

Peaking through the door, I see James kiss her and it makes me happy. I thought I might get jealous but not at all. I feel whole. Like I can actually see a life with them, us!

After I shower, I head back to my room to change, letting James and Jaz know I will be right back for breakfast. As I enter my room with my towel wrapped around me, the smell of Jaz perfume floods my scenes before I feel her hands. She wraps her arms around my waist and whispers in my ear, "I would love to have some you time." She kisses that sweet spot below my ear and I moan and lean into her.

I feel James' hands wrap around us both, "You two have fun, I'd enjoy watching if you're ok with that." He whispers to us both.

"I'm ok with that if Molly is." I can feel Jaz smiling against my neck.

"Uh huh." Is all I seem to get out as Jaz is kissing my neck but James unwraps my towel from me as he backs away.

"We will go at your speed, if you aren't comfortable we'll stop." Jaz tells me as she is guiding me to the bed. I look over to see James sitting at my desk facing us with a smirk on his face, desire in his eyes and a bulge he is palming through his pants from yesterday.

"Jaz, teach me more, please." I say in more of a beg.

Moaning against my neck I can feel her smile, "Gladly, sweetheart."

As she leads me to sit facing her, we start kissing and my hands trail up her side to slowly remove her shirt. Her silky skin is warm and I can feel a slight shiver as I lean in and kiss her stomach. She lifts the shirt over her head and I unsnap her bra and run my tongue over the peak of her nipples as she runs her fingers through my hair. Slowly pulling my head back she leans over to kiss me, moving her hands slowly down my shoulder, onto my chest and cupping my breasts to roll the peak of my nipple between her fingers as I moan into her mouth.

Hearing a low growl from James and we both smile. Letting my hands dip into her pants. I run my hand between her legs, feeling the heat building at her core and she pushes into me more. Unzipping her pants she helps push them down her legs and slowly steps out of them and her panties at the same time. I sense James move out of the corner of my eye and I turn to look as he comes to sit on the corner of the bed.

"I just want to be closer to see.." There is a playful smile and I know he wants more.

"I thought you had to go to work?" Jaz baits him.

"I texted the team lead and said I would be late. He can handle it and you two are more important." He winks at us and I can't help the blush that floods my face and chest.

Jaz turns and smiles at me, "Would you like him to join? I think you will enjoy it more." she asked me with a wicked smile.

I smile, almost unsure, giving her a slight glance. "Do you want him to? You don't want me to yourself?" I am feeling playful today.

"Babe, we have time for one on one. Lets makes this fun for everyone." she leans in and nips at my ear. Glancing over, James has already pulled his dick out and started stroking it. Jaz licks her lips and moans at the sight and I am practically drooling.

"Come help us?" I offer my hand out to him.

I see the feral look in his eye as he stands and drops his pants and takes his shirt off, never taking his eyes off my hand as I reach for Jaz's slit and gently begin to rub my fingers against her clit. Feeling her arousal grow and moisten my finger, moaning and I pull my finger back to lick them.

James mutters to himself more than anyone, "Fuck baby, that's sexy."

Jaz leans to James and pulls him to us but pushes him to kiss me first, "Taste me on her." James does just that without hesitation.He devours my mouth, his tongue fighting to taste every drop of Jaz on my tongue.

Pushing him back so I can take a breath, I reach out and snag Jaz by the wrist and pull her to the bed with me. "You have to tell me what you like, help me make you come for me." I tell her as I push her to lay down and I roll off the bed between her legs kneeling, her legs on either side of me and her perfect pusy open bare to me.

James positions himself beside her for her to suck his throbbing cock, I can see the pre-come at the tip. Right as Jaz sticks her tongue out to lick it, I run my tongue from her soaked opening to the bundle of nerves I know must be throbbing. We all moan for different reasons, and it makes my core tingle with need. I begin to finger myself as I am eating her and watching her suck him. I never knew this could be so arousing.

I begin to rhythmically lick and suck her pussy and gently nibble her clit, moaning against her, "You taste so sweet."

James' voice is harsh and breathy as he says, "Get a good deep lick and kiss me. I need to taste you both."

Barely shaking my head yes, I push my tongue inside her pussy wiggling it as I see her gasp and her back arches off the bed and I pull my tongue out, leaving it out for James. A growl rips through him as I slowly stand and he grabs me by the hair and pulls me to him, "DO. NOT. TEASE. ME."

His mouth slams on mine as I feel Jaz slide down the bed and pull my hips to her to make me ride her face. She hums her approval, "James, you should see how wet she is from eating me." Is all she says before burying her tongue in me and I rock against her moaning as best I can. James keeps kissing me for a moment before he pulls back.

"I want to fuck her as she eats you." His eyes are full of questions and longing and I know I am a goner for these two. I want that more than he knows.

"Please." Is all I manage to get out and Jaz slides out from under me, her chin glistening in my arousal. James licks me off her face before he kisses her.

"Can I?" he asked her, knowing she heard what he said to me.

"Please..." Is all she says before he pulls her onto the bed laying beside me and I shift to straddle her face. James gets off the bed and squats in front of her to lick her slit before he growls and stands. Positioning his cock to the opening of her, "Take all of me." Is all the warning she gets before he seats himself to the hilt in her and she is gripping my thighs for dear life. She is moaning against my pussy as she keeps eating me and I reach down and start massaging her clit. I want to see her come for him.

I only rub her clit a few times before she nips at mine and James' raspy voice makes me look at him, "She is about to come on my cock." He says to me as he leans in to pull me to him for a kiss. "Come baby, come all over your cock so it is ready for our girl." He has a primal need in his eyes as he says it and Jaz does as he says. Coming hard, she moves her head so she can lean up some and I see her squirt, hard, soaking his lower half.

"Fuck Jaz! That's sexy." he smiles his aproval as he keeps his pace fucking her through her orgasm. She squirted three more times before her body began to shake from the after shock.

"Do you want to see Molly come for me now too?" He asks, looking at her trying to catch her breath. She barely shakes her head yes when James looks as me, "Get down here and bend over, I want to watch you clean her pussy while I come." He grabs my hair and guides me to where he wants me and I swear I have never been this turned on by someone handling me this way. James just makes it feel normal and natural.

Bending over in front of him, I use Jaz sated body to brace myself kissing her lower stomach and pelvic before licking her.. James rubs the tip of his cock against my entrance and hums, "You enjoy her eating you as I fucked her didn't you, little lamb." He barely pushes the head in as he pushes my head to Jaz's pussy.

"I told you, I want you to clean her as I fucking come." And he slams all the way into me. Reaching around he starts rubbing my clit and I can feel my core tighten already. I begin licking Jaz as she watches me smiling and riding my mouth for her own pleasure. "Mmm yes baby, clean our pussy." I can hear the arousal in his voice. She brushes hair out of my face and holds it on my way as she rocks her hips against my tongue. I reach down and slide two fingers in her, letting her fuck herself on my hand and face. Moaning, she holds my hair tight and I can feel her pussy tighten on my fingers already.

James rubs my clit and thrust harder, I can feel his grip start to tense. He's close too.

"Come now! I need you to come with me. Both of you" He yells at us both.

I fall over the edge and come harder than last night, feeling all of our orgasm drip down my legs. I press my tongue against Jaz's clit, her inner walls are tight around my fingers and I know she is there with me. At that moment, I curl my fingers up a little to rub the g-spot and she comes again. Squirting, just as I pull my mouth away. James pinches my clit and before I realize what is happening I am squirting on his cock and shaking, trying to stand and fall at the same time. James keeps pumping in me as I ride my orgasm out and Jaz is laying in front of me completely worn out.

Falling onto the bed beside Jaz, both of us on either side, we are all completely spent with grins plastered across our faces. I have never felt bliss like this before.

We all cleaned up and ate our now cold breakfast before we each had to go to work. We all shared locations with each other, they didn't realize how possessive I am but this is just the beginning. I have them and I will kill to keep them.

The feeling is a little strangle as I drive to work but I know it's just because I haven't allowed a woman this close to be in a long time, let alone two, and then talking about Kelly and Bash brought up a lot of old feelings. If Bash is the one my father hired to kill me, I hope he'll hear me out first. He can't think I would have left him for no reason. I loved him before I loved Kelly, and I will always love him, even if he hates me.

After I get on site at Molly's house I check with all my guys and see what is going on and where they need a little help. Before getting to work I check see where my girls are, Jaz is at the realtor office and it looks like Molly is at her companies HQ. I hacked their companies computers and see both their schedules, Jaz has a couple of appointments to show some houses and Molly is at the office for a meeting for a new skyscraper they are building near downtown Kansas City, then she is back to remote working. She only has to go to the office every few weeks so I know where she is most the time, Jaz on the other hand is always running all over meeting clients and showing houses, she is good at what she does though.

The day flew by, I kept busy helping my guys and we got a lot finished. The 5pm timer went off throughout the house, echoing off the new walls but I still heard people working so I yelled for everyone to go home and rest. This is a great crew and I don't mind them getting overtime when they need it but I want them to have a home life also.

Plus I now have two women to tend to, smiling to myself. I start to help clean up.

Shutting the door behind me, I turn towards my truck and see Bill and his brother Kyle standing near it smiling.

"Gentlemen, can I help you with something?" I ask, knowing they wouldn't still be here without a good reason.

Bill clears his throat, "Well sort of, we know the job site is closed but I've known Molly since she was little and I wanted to see if you would allow Kyle and I to stay behind and do the floor in the greenhouse for her. Her dad has done so much for me and I just want to pay it back a little, I'm not looking to be paid but this is your job." He is always so respectful, even though he is twice my age. It's one thing that has always made me respect him more.

"Plus, floors are a pain in the ass and we know what she wants, I think we could knock it out before the sun goes down, so it won't be dark." Kyle pipes in.

I smile at them, "I'll help you and we'll do it a little faster and then dinner is on me boys." I pat them on the shoulders.

Molly doesn't need our help but they wanted to help her and I wanted to help them. They are kind men, they always want to do something a little extra for the houses we do.

"Only one catch, we don't want her to know till she shows up." Bill says, smirking at me.

"What makes you think I could tell her?" I glare at him.

Bill raises an eyebrow and looks at Kyle before they both give me that all knowing stare. "I have seen the way you look at her, just don't hurt her. She has been through a lot. I just want to see her happy. That's all I'm going to say about it." Bill says as he walks around the corner of the house.

"Hmm, so there is high school gossip?" He knows something I don't and I'm not sure I like it.

"Not at all, I know her so I watch out for her since her parents are out of town. She is like a niece to me, and if I can be blunt without making you mad. I have seen the way you watch everything she does when she is here. I think you are a great man James, if you think you can make her happy after her fiancés death, I think you could be good for her. I just want to see her happy."

"I guess I can't fault you for wanting to see her safe." Is the only response I give him as we all head to the greenhouse. I make a mental note to talk to her about her late fiance. I already know everything but she doesn't know that yet. Kyle is already at the greenhouse wiggling the handle, I forgot she locked it for some reason, she never lets me inside, but Bill laughs and mentioned how these old greenhouses have bottom windows that open enough to crawl through as he looks at me. Rolling my eyes as they find one of the windows, crawling through it and I open the door from the inside.

They will get payback for making me crawl through a window, I think to myself. Shaking my head at them laughing outside the door.

The space is beautiful and we all look at it for a moment before I start working on the frame of the floor. Bill was right, the space is big but this won't take but maybe an hour give or take 30 minutes and we'll be done.

An hour and 10 minutes later we are finished and cleaning up. Bill leaves a note for Molly to find and we all turn to head to our vehicles telling the guys to pick what they want for dinner, it's on me.

By the time we finish eating, talking and a couple beers, it's nearly 9 pm and I'm exhausted. Bill and Kyle head home and I check my cameras to see what Molly is doing.

Luckily, Jaz is with Molly so I sent a text.

'I'm headed home to shower and bed, you two have fun, but not too much without me.' I add a wink face.

Molly responds immediately, 'How do you know she is here?'

I just respond with a winky kissy face emoji.Laughing because I know she had to have figured out that I have cameras there.

'Do you have cameras in my parent's house? That's borderline stalking Mr. Wolf.'

'I don't stalk what's already mine, but yes, I do, I have to know you're always safe. Get over it, they aren't going anywhere.'

'Controlling much?'

I chuckle to myself. 'YES'

'Goodnight James, I'll be by MY house tomorrow.' She adds a kissy face emoji.

With that I head home to do just as I said, shower and go to bed.

The next morning seems to come too fast, but I am up and out of the house by 6 am. Heading to the office and checking on messages with Alice, only staying about 30 minutes. Once I leave there I run to get coffee for Molly and Jaz, I heard on the cameras they were coming over this morning and 'stalking' like Molly calls it, I know what they both like to drink.

After getting their coffees, I head to her house to work and see if she has found the greenhouse yet.

As I pull up to the house and Molly's car is just behind me so I pull up the drive. Parking, they pull in beside me and we all get out.

"Good morning ladies. Did you have a good night without me?" I'm smirking and surprised at myself for not being mad. I usually don't share well but with them it's different, I want to share them with each other.

"Oh, we had a GREAT time." Molly is baiting me and I can't help but close the space between us.

"I swear if you don't at least tell me..." Jaz cuts me off before I can finish my statement.

"Tell you? Why would we ruin the fun? I mean, you did admit to having cameras." I see the devious smile as I turn to look at her.

"I went to bed, if I would have known, I would have watched." My voice is deeper than usual, but they bring out an animalistic side of me.

They both start laughing, Molly pushes around me, "All you missed was us drinking wine, celebrating Jaz making another sale and painting each other's toes. Calm your balls, we didn't do anything else, I mean not unless you wanted your toes painted too?"

"Plus you told us to have fun, but we both agreed it would be wrong without you." Jaz rubs my arm as she tells me. She isn't as feisty as Molly, it's a nice balance. Jaz is the sweet to Molly's sour.

"No, I don't want my toes painted. And at least one of you isn't trying to get me riled up before work." I give Molly a pointed glare and all she does is laugh. We all really do fall into a good rhythm together. That makes me calm down, they are really in. That realization almost makes me melt for them. They are absolutely perfect and I couldn't have asked for more.

I look around and make sure no one is outside, pulling them behind my truck, out of view of the house and the team. I leaned in and gave each a kiss, I wanted to start my day off right and that was what I needed to do so.

"Oh, before I forget, I got you both coffee." Heading to the cab, I grab their coffees out and give it to each of them. Molly rolls her eyes, "Of course you know what we drink too."

Jaz laughs, "It's sweet. At least we know he thinks about us." She turns to me, "Thank you." With a wink.

"I appreciate it too, just sucks we can't bring you anything since we haven't stalked you." Molly giggles at Jaz and I.

"Oh but you just haven't found out the fine details." I grin and wink at her. "Ok, I have to work before my guys think I'm just micromanaging. You all do what you need. Dinner, Red Door at 7?"

They both smile and agree.

I turn to go inside with my guys as they go to Molly's car and begin to gather some things.

Molly

After James heads to go inside, Jaz and I get a few things from the car and head back to the greenhouse. Rounding the house, I see the door is propped open, but I know I shut and locked it when I left the other day. As we get closer, I see a note and flowers laying in the open door.

Picking up the flowers and note, I read it to Jaz. 'Your father has done so much for me, I just wanted to pay it forward and let you worry about the rest of the building without worrying about the floor.'

"Sweet but do you know who it is from?" Jaz questions.

Smiling, I turn to look back at the house, to see Bill and his brother Kyle watching from the back door. "Yes, my dad used to help that contractor over there, he and my dad were friends."

Walking towards the house, Bill and Kyle both step off the back deck and I can see they have a questioning look on their faces. Almost like they aren't sure if I'm going to be mad or not.

"Morning Molly, I hope you aren't mad. I just wanted to do something nice and I didn't want to see you get hurt doing it by yourself. We double insulated the floor so you shouldn't have any problems keeping the temperature regulated in there." Bill says to me. I can see the hope in his eyes that I won't be mad.

"I am the farthest from mad. Honestly you did something that I was still trying to figure out how I wanted it done. I can't thank you enough, honestly, but I also can't let you do this for free. I have to pay you something!"

"Sweetheart, your dad has done more than you can ever imagine for me and my family. This was just a little pay it forward to you for some of the things he did for me. If you feel the need to 'pay' me, bring donuts tomorrow. The twist are my favorite." He tells me with a wink and I can't help but laugh.

"Well I think I can pull that off. Maybe some coffee with that too." I say as I turn to look at Kyle, "I know you helped too, so fess up and tell me what donuts you like and I will pick those up too."

He laughs, "Well I don't know what you mean miss Molly, but I do love cinnamon rolls." holding his hands up like he has been caught.

"Ok, I will get those in the morning for you two. Thank you both, so much. Honestly, I appreciate you two doing this for me. You don't know how much I appreciate it."

The men glance between each other and I don't miss the questioning look they exchange. Before I can ask them what that was about, James steps out of the house. "If you two are done talking to Molly and Jaz, maybe we can get back to work?" I don't miss the mischievous grin on his face but then he is gone. Bill and Kyle give me a smile and turn to head back inside.

I head back to the greenhouse where Jaz had made her way inside to look around. Noticing the floors really do look great. They did an amazing job and it was so kind of them. I make a mental note to tell dad what they did, he will be happy to know all his good deeds are coming back full circle.

"What was all that about? I was going to wait but I got nosey and came on in since it was open and all." She grins at me knowing I don't care but I roll my eyes anyways to make her laugh.

"Bill and his brother admitted to doing the floor for me, and they double insulated it, so it should stay temperature controlled better." I bounce a little to see how sturdy they feel.

"Aww that's so sweet, how much are you going to pay them? I mean they did a lot, since they cleaned out the space too. I don't see you letting them go without paying them"

"The only thing they want is donuts." I say laughing. "So I figured I will get them donuts and maybe make James dinner, since I have a feeling he is hiding the fact that he helped. He was late going home last night when he texted us. There is no way he let them stay and him not help."

She lets out a loud gasp, "No? You don't say?" she says sarcastically, and we both start laughing.

After about an hour of walking Jaz through everything I'm wanting to do in the space, we make a plan for the walls. As we walk towards the car. Jaz gets a call about a couple of houses she has listed so I take her to her car and head home to design.

Over the next few weeks, everything went smoothly. My parents called and informed me they are staying longer in Washington, so Jaz and I have been together almost every night. James usually comes by too but if he has been busy he stays home, none of us rest a lot when we are all together. Sometimes we're at my parents house but most nights Jaz and I stay with James, his house feels homey and we all seem comfortable there. His house is beautiful and minimal but it fits him well. I don't know how he is going to handle both Jaz and I, we are vibrant and colorful.

The greenhouse has come so far as well, the walls are finished, my friend from the service was here 3 days ago and we installed the stained-glass wall and windows and the roof is finished. Jaz, James and I shopped for furniture out there and we all agreed, which was a surprise in itself but since the space is big enough, we bought a bunch of fluffy rugs to cover the floor, oversized pillows and floor chairs giving the space a boho vibe that makes my heart happy. James actually liked it and said it allowed for Jaz and I to spend our relaxing days somewhere quiet but he could always join.

Somehow we all really do fit together with ease and it makes me so much comfortable. We agree on more than expected and when we do disagree on something, we tend to find a compromise that works for all of us.

The house is on stage 4, which is the drywall and painting stage and I am so excited. We all sat down and talked and we are all moving into the house as one so I let them help with the paint and design. There is still about 5 weeks till everything is finished, as long as the appliances arrive on time, we got an email that the oven I wanted was delayed but then they gave us a discount and I got a better one.

I have also decided to tell my parents about my relationship and I was surprised they were ok with it. They seemed kind of happy which made this whole thing easier. Mom seemed a little weird about me being in a relationship with two people openly but they agreed that if I'm happy and we can make it work, then they are happy for me and will support me.

James is talking about keeping his house to use as a rental, which we all agree is a wise financial move. He has already paid Jaz's lease on her apartment in full so she can move out whenever she wants. Recently she said she always has this feeling that she is being watched, James probably broke in and installed cameras so she probably was being watched by him. He won't just tell us, we would have to corner him and even then he wouldn't fess up to it unless we caught him but he always smiles when he is avoiding which I have come to notice is a tell that what we are saying is true.

It has been a month since we all started this relationship between us. I think it's more than time to talk with Jaz about James' past. I just hope she isn't upset that we didn't tell her sooner. Honestly we fell into a great momentum and I haven't thought about it all that much but for some reason I get the feeling that we all need to have this talk sooner rather than later. We agreed to be honest and open with each other. It's time to hold up the entire deal.

I don't even ask James, I know he won't argue, so I open our group chat, we rarely text one-on-one, it's part of our open honest communication agreement we made last week.

Opening the chat I named 'Paris' for the Eiffel Tower. Jaz and I thought it was hilarious. James rolled his eyes but he was smiling, he knows the visual image is true.

"Hey babes, let's do dinner in tonight." I add a kiss wink emoji before sending.

Jaz replies first, "Sounds good to me, I'll grab the wine and more scotch for James."

James was the last to reply. "I'm good with that, head to my house and I'll go by the store and get something for dinner along with the stuff to make cheesecake for dessert."

Smiling, I put my phone down only to have it buzz. James sent only me a message.

"It's time to talk, isn't it?"

"Yes babe it is. It's only right." I sigh as I hit send. I know this is a lot for him to talk about.

He doesn't answer. I know he just needed to know how to approach the night.

A s the day comes to an end I help my crew with some minor clean up before heading to the store for dinner.

I decided steak and baked potatoes are good with cheesecake. Jaz loves a good grilled steak and since it's going to be a rough night, I want to cater to what she likes. Molly will eat about anything so I know she won't care. I pick out three New York strips with perfect marbling, grab all the toppings for the potatoes and some extra charcoal. I make sure to pick up the cheesecake ingredients. The girls like plain cheesecake so I don't need to get cherries or strawberries for topping but I do make sure to grab fresh strawberries and champagne. I know the girls got wine but champagne goes well with the cheesecake.

Once I get home, the girls are already there and perched in their usual spot on an oversized chair on the back porch having some wine. I love coming home to them like this, it feels right. They're curled up in the chair together, laughing and talking about their days when Molly speaks a little louder.

"Hey there handsome, you know you're slacking on the sneaking in thing. We know you're behind us." Jaz starts to laugh at Molly's declaration.

"I wasn't trying to sneak in. I just enjoy seeing you two here, I was just soaking in the moment. My apologies for being sentimental for once." I can't help the smile on my face. "Since I've been called out though, I guess it's time to start dinner. New York strips and baked potatoes with cheesecake sound good with you two?"

Jaz turns and gives me a smile that melts every wall that I built. "Well, you sure know the way to my heart, don't you?"

"Hey now, what about the way to my heart?" Molly laughs leaning against Jaz.

"Oh don't worry. I know the secret path to yours and we will get there later." Jaz leans over and softly says to Molly as she kisses her.

"Fuck me, keep that up and we will skip dinner and go straight to bed." I groan. These two keep me hard most of the day and as much as I enjoy it, I do need to have this talk with Jaz.

I head to drop off the charcoal at the grill, leaning down kissing both the girls as I pass. There is an empty bottle of wine beside them, so I know they have been here at least an hour. Molly has a mischievous look in her eye and I know she is in a mood to play, but I cut her a look and she pouts. Fuck, she is so cute when she pouts. I was happy her parents were ok with the situation we have here, it made things a lot easier on all of us. I was worried about it at first but I think they can see how happy she is and it stirs feelings I forgot about till these two.

Jaz stands and takes the potatoes, "I'll do these, since the last two times you did it they weren't fully cooked or burnt. I prefer cooked potatoes versus raw or bricks." She tells me with a wink and Molly swats her ass as she saunters away giggling like a kid.

"I'll set the table, you want a scotch while you're grilling?" Molly asks as she follows Jaz into the house.

"Sounds like a plan. Thank you." I told her. We really have fallen into a great rhythm and now that we're all officially together, I couldn't imagine it any other way. I haven't been this happy in years.

Jaz starts the potatoes, while Molly makes us all drinks and gets out the stuff to set the table and I start the grill.

Molly walks out with my drink in hand and a smile on her face that can only be described as a mix of lust and satisfaction. Handing me my drink, she gets up on her toes to give me a kiss and I lean down to accommodate her. "Thank you for making this about her. It means a lot to me." Is all she says before she heads back inside to get the dishes and silverware.

I never used the back porch area before the girls but we spend so much time here I gave them my credit card and let them pick some things that make them feel more at home. My place was minimal before them, and it still is now but the little touches they added make it feel more of a home. They bought an outdoor sectional we can all sit on with an oversized chair, which is their favorite, an outdoor table that seats 6 and some "mood lighting" for the porch. I thought it was silly but all together, it works and it makes them happy, which makes me happy. The last thing they bought was delivered last week and I was surprised to come home to the girls smiling like the little devils they are. Leading me to the back porch they showed me my surprise. They had ordered me a top of the line grill/smoker and I couldn't have been happier. Cooking in the kitchen isn't my thing, but grilling, I can do this all day everyday and the food is always perfect, just don't ask me to do anything with the stove, I will burn the place down.

I can't wait to see what they do when the house is completely finished. We all agreed we will move in together and since I'm me, I ordered a custom bed that could fit us all, and 3 more if we wanted. I don't plan on sharing them though, I just wanted the extra space since Jaz and I tend to toss and turn a lot. That's the surprise I have for them when the house is done, the bed is waiting in my storage unit till it's time.

Once the potatoes are finished, the steaks are just finishing as Jaz is bringing them out. I cooked them low and slow to keep the juice and flavor in them. Luckily we all eat them about medium done so I don't have to do anything special. I give them one last brush of garlic butter before Molly brings the plates over for them each.

Taking them back to the table, I can't help but smack her ass as she turns from me, laughing and yelping as she jumps and runs aways, I can't help but laugh also. As Jaz comes out to set the potatoes on the table, I do the same to her and her reaction is the same as Mollys. They make me laugh harder than I think I ever have.

"Couldn't get one without the other." I wink as I sit down at my spot and the girls each take a spot on either side of me.

We all make our plates and make small talk about the day for a few minutes before Jaz starts to eye Molly and I.

"Ok, what's going on? I can feel it in my bones. This isn't one of our normal meals." Jaz says as she gives us both a worried look.

Taking a deep breath and slowly letting it out, I turn to look at her. "Well, you and I never had our talk and that's not fair. We all have fallen into this so easily and I don't want to lose either of you. So it's time I tell you the truth and if you want to walk away, speaking for myself, I will understand." I grab her hand and give it a small squeeze. This is going to hurt if she walks away.

We keep eating as I tell Jaz everything. She is patient and listens, just as Molly did and I'm grateful because it gives me hope. Once I am finished telling Jaz everything Molly is the first one to speak.

"I know this is a lot, but you deserve to know. I choose to be ok with all this, and yes, it would hurt if you weren't but I would understand and I would hope that we could still be friends. Though I won't lie, I'm hoping we can all get through this as one like we have been doing." Hearing the worry in her voice hurts and I want to make it all better but I know there is nothing I can do to help her.

Jaz is just finishing her last bite as she sets her fork and knife down. Taking a breath and a sip of wine, she sets forward and looks between us both before speaking.

"So let me first off say, I understand why you're hiding and I think we can all get through this because, to me at least, there is nothing to get through. You both are mine and I'm yours. Second, if we are going to get into honesty, I need to tell you that both I have a secret too." She ducks her head slightly in shame. Something feels off but I can't put my finger on it.

I see her expression change to almost fear as she looks at me and it breaks my heart. There is nothing she could tell me that would make me not want her or Molly.

Reaching over I grab both their hands, "You can tell us anything. I'm in this and nothing is going to change that." I tell her as I bring her hands up to kiss her knuckles. Molly rests her hand on my leg, gently rubbing and I know it's her way or agreeing.

"I am from Boston also." Is all Jaz says at first and I can feel her stiffen. Boston is a big city, there are a lot of people from there.

"Six years ago, I was out for an evening run. I always ran the Weeks Footbridge because it is beautiful out there." Her eyes start to gloss over with tears and I already know what she is about to say. I knew something about her was familiar but it wasn't like I knew her, I passed her of an evening when I was there to see Kelly at that exact bridge. I can feel my stomach bottom out but I need this.

"I remember seeing the same couple meeting out there a few times a week, and I always thought it was cute but I never paid attention. James, I'm so sorry I didn't know!" The tears are falling like rivers now. Squeezing her hand, I can feel the first tear fall. She knows something that I wanted an answer to and that I'm afraid of also.

"One night, I was running as I saw him leaving, well I guess now I know you were leaving. You walked away and I saw you cut into a small side trail before I saw three men come out of the bushes. It happened so fast I could barely stop and hide. They hit her a few times and then as she was crying, one of them squatted to get closer to her face, I barely heard him over my breathing but I heard him tell her 'Caleb wanted his son back and a Russian whore isn't going to stand in the way.' When he stood back up he shot her in the head but before I could process what happened I got up and ran. I knew they saw me, I could hear them yelling at me and someone shot at me but I ran as fast as I could. I made it back to my apartment and immediately started packing. I also had a stalker back then, he somehow always finds me, this is the longest I have been in one since then. I legally changed my name to not only hide from my stalker but also those other men, they scared me to the core and I was afraid they would find me. Before I changed my name I was

Jazmine Belus." She is crying and shaking and I'm tense and crying also. I knew something happened but I never knew what.

Standing up, Jaz jumped back like she was scared of me and it made me pause because it hurt for her to look at me like that. I glance over at Molly who is also crying, she doesn't know what to say to either of us. I'm not upset, I don't blame her at all, hell I don't know what to say, so I drop to my knees in front of Jaz.

"Baby, I'm so sorry you saw that but thank you for giving me an answer I never knew. I'm not mad or upset and I promise they won't hurt you. I'll kill them all before they hurt either of you." I tell her as I hold her knees and kiss her legs. I am still crying but I hope she understands how serious I am.

Before I can think to move, I hear her voice, low and timid and I hate it but I listen, "If I would have realized it was you I would have told you. I never knew and I never expected to run into someone from there, here."

I give the best smile I can at the moment, "You had no way of knowing, I always kept a hood on." I stand and kiss her tear soak cheeks before pulling my chair closer to her, "But I do want to know a few things. Can you tell me what the men looked like, I think I know already but I want to be sure. And do you know who your stalker was? I want to find him before he finds you."

"When it comes to the men, I only remember one, he scared me the most. He had the most deranged look in his eye, like he was getting joy out of what he was doing. He was at least 6'2" with overly toned muscles like he was on steroids, jet black greasy hair and a trinity knot tattoo on the top of his left hand." She says hoping that was something and it definitely is.

"Marcus Flanigan. My fathers right hand man. And you're right he is completely unhinged. He killed my mom when I was 8 because she refused to have sex with him and when she told my dad, he let Marus rape and murder her." I'm nauseous by the thought, my father and

Marus fed off each other's psychopathic tendencies and were known for doing things like that. That was one of many reasons I never wanted to be a part of that life.

"Holy fuck, saying I'm sorry isn't even close to the feelings I have." Jaz says and I feel Molly come up beside us. Still being quiet, she sits in a chair between us just taking both our hands.

"My stalker on the other hand, I have no idea. I started getting flowers and notes at my apartment about 8 months before things happened," she winced at me before continuing after I nod and kiss her hand. "He never hurt or made threats against me. He more so watched EVERYTHING. He would text me and remind me to lock my door or shut my blinds because 'he didn't want anyone else to watch me.' But something made me feel like he knew more or was into more than he wanted me to know. It was just a feeling though.I don't know why, yes he stalked me and watched me but I never felt like he would have hurt me. I still have all the notes he sent me, they are in a lock box in my car. I don't know why I just felt better having them close. I can get them if you want."

"I'd like to see them, I doubt I will be of any help but it will give me a feeling for the guy." I tell her and she stands.

"One last thing. I always have this feeling when he shows back up. I think he found me again. I can't explain it but I just feel like I'm being watched and I saw a single rose petal on my car this afternoon. It may be nothing and I chalked it up to that but he always left pink roses, and this was a pink rose petal. Maybe I'm paranoid, but I figured I would let you know." She shrugs as she turns to head into the house to get her car keys.

Molly jumps up, "Well, I for one am NOT taking any chances, I will go to the car with you." She takes Jaz hand and kisses her, "We're all in this together."

As they walk through the house I set back and take a breath. A twig snaps behind my fence and I jump to my feet. Fuck I'm paranoid now too. Animals are always walking around back there, hell last week I saw five deer. Shaking my head, I start to clean up dinner and grab the cheesecake.

I am just setting the cheesecake down when the girls walk in and Jaz is holding a small stack of notes on what looks like flower shop notecards. She holds them out and as I take them she kisses me, soft and quick but passionately.

"'Thank you for not being mad. I love you two too much to hurt you, please know that." As she finishes her sentence she gasps, "OMG. I'm sorry, I-I didn't mean like.."

I cut her off, "Do not apologize! I love you too. I didn't think I could again but you both changed that and I won't let that go." I kiss her more ravenously and I feel her melt against me.

Turning to Molly, I reach out and pull her close to us both, "And I love you also." Kissing her with just as much need.

Molly smiles and rolls her eyes, "Thanks for putting me on the spot." She giggles as I pinch her ass. "But I will say thank you to you both. You both have helped me realize I can love, and I DO love you both. I didn't think I would be this happy after Kenneth, but then you two flipped my world upside down and sideways and I couldn't be happier. I love you both!" She kisses us both and we all fall back into our easy dynamic.

Clearing my throat and pulling away, "Let me look at these while you eat cheesecake before I drag you both inside and have my way with you." I wink at Jaz as she hands them to me.

I set down and look at the first note, I freeze and my hands start to shake. It's his handwriting. I would know it anywhere.

James

I have to be imagining it.

    I know this handwriting has to be different.

I was just talking about my past.

This can't be real.

Staring at the letters, nausea making my stomach roll and my head spin. The handwriting doesn't change the longer I look at them and I know without a doubt who her stalker is. Bash is her stalker, but Bash isn't the stalking type. He can get anyone he wants. I've known him since we were about five. He was my first love.

My mind is reeling and I'm frozen with memories of him and I. I have missed him but refused to think about that time. I couldn't go back, there was no use thinking about what I couldn't have.

It was a long weekend, Bash has been with someone all weekend so I've either been stuck with my father 'helping in the business' or running off to Weeks Footbridge to see Kelly. It's the only place we can go since no one in my family knows of that spot, it's not their territory.

Knocking on Bash's door, he doesn't verbally answer me, he just unlocks it and walks away. His dad is the contractor for my father, though his dad is nice, I don't see how he tolerates mine, but Bash and I grew up together and through time, we became more. He is my first love, even with Kelly, when I need to get some stress out, I turn to Bash. We have an understanding, mainly because my father would kill us both if he knew what we really mean to the other.

"You really should check to see who is at the door before you unlock it dumbass." I tell him as I walk into his apartment.

"Fucker, I seen you coming. You know I watch cameras so why do I need to check when I know it is you." He rolls his eyes at me.

"Where were you all weekend? You don't usually go MIA." I ask only slightly annoyed.

"I wasn't MIA, all you had to do was call and I would have been there. Don't be dramatic."

"Really, you know what I mean. What's going on with you? Better yet who is she?" I smirk at him. I know him too well to know it has to be a woman.

"Her name is Jazmine. It's new so you don't need to know anything more right now." He wraps me in a hug and gives me a kiss. "Did you need some of my attention this weekend and get all pissy because I was busy?"

"Actually yes, he was a different prick this weekend and you know I can't blow off steam with Kelly the way I need to. You know that's only something you can handle, or give." I tell him as I push him back to the bed.

"Yea, dad called and said Caleb was foul this weekend. That's why I disappeared, well part of the reason at least. I didn't think you would get that backlash, sorry." Bash winces a little as I rip his pants from him. He knows how I am when I'm in these moods.

"Well, I did but not too much. You know I want nothing to do with his 'business' so I needed a release. Later we will talk about this Jazmine woman. Now I need you." I give him a devilish grin as I see he is already hard for me.

Molly is shaking me and I snap back from the memory. Adjusting my cock in my pants, I turn to Jaz and Molly.

"I know who your stalker is. I didn't put two and two together till I saw the writing and it just clicked, it all makes sense now." I tell Jaz. Almost breathless from the memory.

"What? Who?" I can't tell if she is excited or nervous.

"Bash, my first love. I told you we were more than friends. I loved him and I was remembering one bad weekend I had 'helping' my father and he was gone all weekend. I was pissed at him for leaving me for a woman. He told me he was seeing a Jazmine and it was still new so he wouldn't tell me more."

"Hold on. What? Your best friend/lover Bash, was stalking Jaz?" Molly asks, obviously trying to play catch up to the bomb I just dropped.

"I'd know his writing anywhere. It is the most unique handwriting I have ever seen. A mix of English and Italian, his family is from Italy. He spent a lot of time there so when he writes, I could always tell it was him." Holding up the notes, "This is definitely his writing."

"Ok, so if he is my stalker and by chance, he found me, that means he found you too. Is this good, bad or really fucking bad?" Jaz's face is etched with concern.

"Honestly, I don't know. I didn't tell him I was leaving, I just left. I knew if I told him, he would try and leave with me and my father would burn everyone and everything to find us. He may be pissed. I don't know but I need to talk to him." I try to explain but I am still reeling from this realization.

"How are you going to talk to him though? Wouldn't you be outing yourself by contacting him?" Molly asked me.

At that moment, a person jumped the fence and had a gun trained on us.

"Well you won't have to look for me long, love. Long time Damion, or is it James now?" I know his gun is trained to the back of my head. Jaz and Molly gasp and huddle together. I don't flinch, if he is as pissed as he sounds, this is a bad situation and sudden movements will set him off.

Slowly I turn around and there he is, less than 3 feet away pointing a gun at my head, and he looks pissed.

"Six fucking years I have been looking for you! Your father has a $20million reward out on your head. But here you are, as I'm watching you kiss MY girl and my girl kissing MY man! We promised forever,

WHAT THE ACTUAL FUCK DAMION?!" He is screaming at me, but I feel the pain in his words. This could work to my benefit.

I open my mouth to try and explain, then I hear the gun go off. Everything starts to go black and I hear Jaz and Molly scream my name and I fall to the ground.

Want to know what happens next? Does Bash kill James? What happens to Molly and Jaz?

Book 2 in The Fatal Contractors Duet

Tangled

Thank you so much for reading Bare. I hope you enjoyed reading it as much as I enjoyed writing it.

If you would like to leave me a personal message, feel free to email me at

<u>authoronyxhart@gmail.com</u>